"It's been a long time, Abby."

She jerked to [...]
As she slowly [...] he
shadows. He v[...]
touch.

"I wasn't sure if you'd talk to me." Jack studied her.

Before leaving home, Abby had vowed that he'd never know how hurt she'd been. "It's been eight years. I hear you're a celebrity now." How often had he told her that he was going to be a world champion? "You got what you wanted."

He'd wanted her. And he'd wanted the rodeo. Logic had told him he couldn't have both. He stuck a hand in his jeans pocket to keep from touching one of the soft silky strands framing her heart-shaped face. "The boy in the car—"

Abby raised her chin. "He's my son." *Our son.* Years ago, she'd buried her secret so no one would guess the truth—she'd had Jack's baby!

Dear Reader,

As you head for your favorite vacation hideaway, don't forget to bring along some Special Edition novels for sensational summertime reading!

This month's THAT'S MY BABY! title commemorates Diana Whitney's twenty-fifth Silhouette novel! *I Now Pronounce You Mom & Dad,* which also launches her FOR THE CHILDREN miniseries, is a poignant story about two former flames who conveniently wed for the sake of their beloved godchildren. Look for book two, *A Dad of His Own,* in September in the Silhouette Romance line, and book three, *The Fatherhood Factor,* in Special Edition in October.

Bestselling author Joan Elliott Pickart wraps up her captivating THE BACHELOR BET series with a heart-stirring love story between an amnesiac beauty and a brooding doctor in *The Most Eligible M.D.* The excitement continues with *Beth and the Bachelor* by reader favorite Susan Mallery—a romantic tale about a suburban mom who is swept off her feet by her very own Prince Charming. And fall in love with a virile *Secret Agent Groom,* book two in Andrea Edwards's THE BRIDAL CIRCLE series, about a shy Plain Jane who is powerfully drawn to her mesmerizing new neighbor.

Rounding out this month, Jennifer Mikels delivers an emotional reunion romance that features a rodeo champ who returns to his hometown to make up for lost time with the woman he loves... and the son he never knew existed, in *Forever Mine.* And family secrets are unveiled when a sophisticated lady melts a gruff cowboy's heart in *A Family Secret* by Jean Brashear.

I hope you enjoy each of these romances—where dreams come true!

Best,

Karen Taylor Richman
Senior Editor

Please address questions and book requests to:
Silhouette Reader Service
U.S.: 3010 Walden Ave., P.O. Box 1325, Buffalo, NY 14269
Canadian: P.O. Box 609, Fort Erie, Ont. L2A 5X3

JENNIFER MIKELS

FOREVER MINE

Published by Silhouette Books

America's Publisher of Contemporary Romance

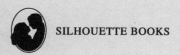

SILHOUETTE BOOKS

ISBN 0-373-24265-4

FOREVER MINE

Visit us at www.romance.net

Printed in U.S.A.

Books by Jennifer Mikels

Silhouette Special Edition

A Sporting Affair #66
Whirlwind #124
Remember the Daffodils #478
Double Identity #521
Stargazer #574
Freedom's Just Another Word #623
A Real Charmer #694
A Job for Jack #735
Your Child, My Child #807
Denver's Lady #870
Jake Ryker's Back in Town #929
Sara's Father #947
Child of Mine #993
Expecting: Baby #1023
Married...With Twins! #1054
Remember Me? #1107
A Daddy for Devin #1150
The Marriage Bargain #1168
Temporary Daddy #1192
Just the Three of Us #1251
Forever Mine #1265

Silhouette Romance

Lady of the West #462
Maverick #487
Perfect Partners #511
The Bewitching Hour #551

JENNIFER MIKELS

is from Chicago, Illinois, but resides now in Phoenix, Arizona, with her husband, two sons and a shepherd-collie. She enjoys reading, sports, antiques, yard sales and long walks. Though she's done technical writing in public relations, she loves writing romances and happy endings.

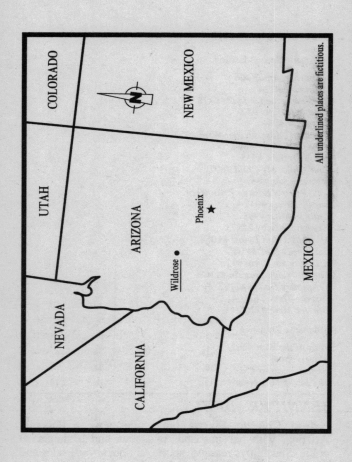

All underlined places are fictitious.

Chapter One

"Mom, you're frowning."

Abby Dennison brought forth a smile for her son's sake. On the passenger seat beside her, he'd been chattering about the ranch, about seeing cattle and horses. She'd listened absently, her mind troubled ever since she and Austin had landed at Sky Harbor Airport in Phoenix. Until minutes ago, the drive to Sam McShane's ranch for the wedding between him and her aunt had been ordinary. Along with nightfall, rain had begun. Now it pounded at the ground.

"Boy, it's raining harder, Mom."

She gripped the steering wheel and kept her eyes on the beam of light before her. She'd heard anxiousness in his voice. "The angels are bowling again," she said lightly about the rumble of thunder.

''How far do we have to go?'' It amazed her that he hadn't asked that question before this. At seven, he tended to run out of patience quickly.

''Not far.'' She spoke louder, to be heard over the rain hammering a beat on the roof of the car. She might have stayed in Phoenix for the night if she'd had an idea of a storm brewing. But monsoons swept abruptly through the desert in late August, and she'd already been on the interstate when the rain had started. ''Want to sing?'' she asked, hoping to distract him from the thunder and lightning.

''What song?''

She started singing a popular country song that was played so often on the radio that Austin knew all the words.

Another rumble of thunder, this one directly over them, made Abby gasp. This trip definitely wasn't starting out well. But then, she'd worried about returning to the ranch ever since her aunt's phone call six months ago.

An exuberant and optimistic woman, Laura Gallagher had sounded more cheerful than usual when she'd announced that she was marrying Sam McShane in the summer. Seeing Sam was no problem, but how would it be to be near Jack again? Abby wondered.

''Whoa!'' Austin yelled.

Abby saw fingers of lightning stab at the peak of a distant mountain.

''Did you see that, Mom?''

''Yes, I saw it.'' The storm could have waited

until they'd reached the lodge. Getting caught in a rainstorm on a busy street in Boston meant inconvenience and being late to arrive somewhere. In Arizona, danger always lurked nearby when the rain drenched the dry ground and filled sandy washes, and water overflowed onto the roads.

"Mom, should I call Sam uncle after he marries Aunt Laura?"

"That's up to you. Do you want to?"

"I don't know yet." He shifted topics in the same breath. "Aunt Laura said he's a rodeo champion."

"No, Sam isn't." Abby peered hard to see through a sheet of rain. "His son, Jack, is."

As lightning lit the dark two-lane road, Austin strained against the seat belt and leaned forward to peer out the rain-splattered window. "How come you know them?"

"I used to work at their ranch." Eight years ago, needing money for her last semester of college, she'd grabbed a plane in Houston and had taken a summer job waiting on tables at Sam's dude ranch. She viewed that as the most adventurous thing she'd ever done in her life. At first, she'd had difficulty dealing with the dust and the heat, and had almost quit the job. But the people had made her want to stay. She'd liked everyone she'd met, especially the owner's son.

"Don't you like it here anymore, Mom?"

His question alerted Abby to the frown she was wearing again. "I like it." Before she left, she'd loved the country living, would have been content to stay there the rest of her life. "Sometimes it's sad to come back to a place you've been, a place you have memories of."

"Why?"

"Because it's not the same as it was before," she offered as an explanation.

His eyebrows bunched, an indication her adult logic made no sense to him.

"I worked there and made friends with other people who worked there," she said. "Some of them are gone. That makes me sad." She'd asked Sam about Lili Gentry, a thin, sharp-tongued woman who'd been in charge of the dining-room kitchen, and she'd learned that Lili had died five years ago. The woman had been tough, a taskmaster to work for, but fair, and caring.

"There are cowboys there, huh?" he asked, the excitement in his voice raising a level.

One cowboy in particular. "Yes." Slowing the rental car, she negotiated a turn onto the dirt road that paralleled a stream.

Headlights projected a narrow tunnel of light. Thunder rumbled in the distance. A crack of lightning resounded a second before it snapped at the ground. A downpour raged. As rain blocked her from seeing the road, she flicked on her signal lights and eased the car onto the narrow shoulder. She didn't need to land in the ditch. Only a fool kept driving.

"Are we stopping here?"

"It's getting too hard to drive, Austin." In her

rearview mirror, she saw the dim headlights of another vehicle, a truck, judging by the height of the beams, stopping behind them.

Abby squinted out the side window at streams of rain running down the glass and scanned the inky darkness, trying to determine how far they were from the ranch. If she had a clear view, she'd be able to see the white adobe buildings with their red tile rooftops. To one side of the three-story main lodge were several cottages and a motel-style building with half a dozen rooms.

The last time she'd seen the ranch, several guests had been strolling along the flagstone walkway that led to the pool, and beyond that the golf course, while other guests had lingered near the corral to wait for horses. Those were the images she remembered of the Double M. But her memories were wrapped around Jack McShane. Always Jack.

She heard the slam of the truck door and fixed her stare on the side mirror. She saw no one, then like an apparition, the hazy outline of a man appeared at the end of her car.

"Mom, are we scared?"

Sound confident, she reminded herself. She slanted a smile at him. "Not at all." No doubt one of the ranch hands had braked behind her.

Austin looked unconvinced. "Okay."

During the time she'd answered him, the man's feet had eaten up the ground. Peripherally, she saw him beside her before he rapped on the window, before she inched down her window to talk to him.

"Are you okay?"

Abby stared, simply stared. Breath lodged in her throat. She wasn't ready for this moment. Tall, broad-shouldered, he stood beside her car with rain dripping from the brim of his Stetson. She knew the face with its high cheekbones and strong, square jaw as well as her own. She'd hoped she would feel nothing, but felt reluctant to make contact with the piercing blue eyes that used to melt her. "Hi, Jack."

"Abby?"

She drew a deep breath. During the passing years, she'd convinced herself that she never wanted to see him again. He'd been the love of her life, her first love, the man she'd lost her innocence to, the man who'd owned her heart—the man who'd dumped her.

She met his eyes now, eyes that appeared dark, shadowed by the mantle of night and the hat's brim. He squinted as if he was trying to see her better. Then he bent forward to peer into the car, see past her, and she realized he was staring at Austin. Could he tell? she wondered.

"Let's get you out of the rain. I'll lead in the truck and keep you on the road," he said, making eye contact with her again. "All you have to do is follow my taillights to stay out of the ditch."

A temptation coursed through her to U-turn, hop a plane, go home. Silly actions. He meant nothing to her anymore. She was simply nervous, worried she'd reveal a secret she'd harbored for eight years.

"Mom, who was that?"

Abby marshaled her thoughts back to the moment. *Your father.* ''That's Jack McShane, Sam's son.'' That was all Austin needed to know. More explanation would have made no sense.

She waited until Jack eased his truck from the shoulder, then followed, staying close to the taillights of the horse trailer. She supposed this was the easiest way for this meeting to happen.

She hadn't known what she'd expected. She'd been hurt rather than angry years ago. He'd left the ranch suddenly one night, left her without even a goodbye. In retrospect, she knew it was her own fault for having expected too much. He'd never lied to her, never made promises. He'd told her no marriage. Marriage and kids usually went hand in hand. He'd wanted neither. But young, foolish, she'd thought he would change his mind.

On the road ahead of her, he passed through the wooden archway that announced the Double M Ranch. As the brake lights on the horse trailer flashed, Abby stopped her car. Out the opened window, he arm-signaled her to go straight to the lodge. He turned right.

''Where's he going, Mom?''

''To the stables.'' *To the place where your father kissed me for the first time.*

''There's Aunt Laura,'' Austin yelled when the buildings were visible.

Standing on the well-lit porch, her aunt, a trim, petite woman in her mid-fifties, was dressed in jeans and a western shirt and a Stetson. She looked so much like Abby's mother had that Abby felt a small twinge of grief return. It was almost as if she were looking at her mother instead of her aunt. Before Austin unbuckled his seat belt, she'd scurried down the steps with an umbrella. The next few moments included a rush of hugs from her aunt and Sam.

"How's my best boy?" Laura asked, enveloping Austin in her arms.

His face scrunched against her body with her exuberant hug, he raised his eyes to her and gave her his best smile. "Aunt Laura, can I ride a horse?"

Glowing, her blond hair shining beneath the porch light, Laura looked elated. "Of course you can," she assured him without a moment's hesitation.

Abby decided to take charge. "We'll see." She didn't need mind-reading abilities to guess that her aunt planned to indulge Austin during the next two weeks.

"I'm glad you both came," Sam said, trailing them with the luggage. Tall and barrel-chested, he wasn't a handsome man, but he had an infectious laugh and a compelling smile that reached warm blue eyes. "It's great seeing you again. A lot has changed since you were here before." Lovingly he looked at her aunt. "I've got you to thank for that."

Abby saw the depth of pleasure in his face. Last Christmas, when she and Austin had left Boston to spend the holiday with her aunt in Houston, they'd gone to a horse auction and had run into Sam. Abby had introduced him to her aunt. And Cupid had taken over.

"We're going to have a lot of fun." Sam touched Austin's shoulder to let him know he was part of that "we." "And we'll have to find you a hat real soon."

Austin looked thrilled, flashing a smile that revealed a missing tooth. "Mom, he means a *cowboy* hat for me."

"Absolutely." Laura draped an arm around Austin's slim shoulder and urged him toward the door. "I'll show you to your rooms."

Inside, everything looked as Abby remembered it. They crossed the massive timbered lobby with its wood-beamed cathedral ceiling and plank flooring. Above a flagstone fireplace hung an enormous Indian weave. Grouped near a wall of floor-to-ceiling windows that offered a view of the desert and the distant mountains were soft, cushiony, western-style sofas. To the left were several round wooden tables with captain's chairs that circled a piano.

"Abby, you are happy for me, aren't you?" Laura asked softly.

Abby couldn't have been happier. She'd always liked Sam. In fact, she'd envisioned him as her father-in-law eight years ago. "Of course I am."

Their arms hooked, they climbed the heavy oak staircase to the second floor.

When they reached the hall, Sam was opening a door. "I hope you like your rooms," he said to Abby.

Warm and welcoming, the room was large and cream-colored with a glass door that opened onto a terrace. Like the living-room section, the adjacent bedroom had whitewashed furniture. It contained a king-size bed, a writing desk, a chest of drawers and another chair. An adjoining door on the opposite side of the suite led to another bedroom, similarly furnished.

Austin sat on the bed, and bounced only once as Abby sent him a quick look.

"This is lovely," Abby assured Sam, returning to the living room and touching the sofa with its dark blue and tan Southwestern design.

"I'll see both of you later then." Instead of looking at them, Sam glanced toward the window. "It's still raining."

"Now, don't worry." Abby's aunt patted Sam's forearm. "I'm sure he's fine. We thought Jack would be here by now," she explained.

"He is here," Abby said. "He stopped on the road to lead us in. He's probably at the stables."

Relief softened the lines in Sam's face. "Good. I'll go find him." In passing, he let his hand touch Laura's.

Abby's aunt waited only until the door closed behind him and they were alone. "He worried Jack might not come."

"Why?"

"They aren't as close as they used to be."

Since that night? Abby wondered. Ray, the ranch foreman, had told her Jack had left. He'd had a fight with Sam and left. No one knew why. "Did Sam tell you what happened?" she asked Laura, feeling sad for them. Because her own father had been absent from most of her life, she'd envied Jack's close relationship with his father.

Laura whisked past her to close the curtain. "Actually, no."

"Doesn't that bother you?"

"Yes, but I will not be meddlesome. Whatever's wrong is between them, Abby."

Abby wouldn't have backed off so easily. If she were about to marry someone, she'd want to know why a strain existed in his relationship with his son. Maybe one of them should find out, she decided.

"You aren't sorry you came, are you?" Laura asked.

Seeing the distress in her aunt's pale blue eyes, Abby offered her a quick assurance. "I'm honored to be your maid of honor."

"Abigail, no diversions." She grabbed Abby's hands. "We haven't discussed this, but I have to ask. Are you really all right about seeing Jack again?" Laura asked in a low voice, with a glance in Austin's direction to be certain he couldn't hear.

"I'm fine." She had to be. She'd have to be around him for the next two weeks.

"I thought you might feel uncomfortable." Her aunt's fair eyebrows knit. "You've said very little to me about Jack, but I know he was important to you once."

"That was a long time ago, Aunt Laura." She mustered up her most convincing smile. "I was still in college, twenty-one."

"Yes, I know." Her eyes searched Abby's face as if she was trying to read the truth in her words. If she'd wanted to say something to her niece about Austin, she didn't as he bounded into the room. "I'll let you get settled in."

Abby maintained her smile until the door shut. Behind her, she heard the theme song of a Disney movie coming from the television. With Austin occupied for the moment, she sank to the closest chair to relax. The tension she'd come here with had intensified.

If she closed her eyes, if she let her mind wander, she could still feel the caress of Jack's hands when the headiness of lovemaking had enveloped them. From the first moment he'd directed that blue gaze at her on a warm May evening when she'd met him at the airport, she'd known he was the one for her. Then the next day, he'd strolled into the ranch dining room where she'd been waiting on tables. Every girl working at the ranch had ogled him. Handsome, fun, rich, he'd had a reputation for winning in rodeos and with the ladies.

She'd tried not to act silly, dreamy-eyed, about the tanned cowboy with the tousled brown hair, but he'd flashed that smile of white, even teeth at her. She'd smiled back, then had gone on working.

Friends had gathered around her when she entered the kitchen for her orders. He'd smiled at *her,* they'd gushed with youthful giddiness. It took effort, but Abby had managed to act indifferent. Plates in hands, she'd reentered the dining room. He'd still been there, still smiling, still staring at her.

That had been the beginning. They'd been inseparable during the next four months. On the night he'd taken off without a goodbye, without a look back, he'd made it clear that he'd never loved her. But she'd foolishly loved him with all her heart. She'd cried, as if mourning a death.

"Mom?"

That one word snapped her back to reality, a reminder that she wasn't that giddy young girl who'd let emotion lead her. Mothers needed to keep their feet firmly planted.

"Mom, I left my comic books in the car," Austin said with a little whine. "Can I go get them?"

"I'll get them." Rather than unpack her umbrella for a run to the car, she dug her windbreaker from a suitcase. "I'm going to lock the door. You know the rule."

His eyes fixed on the television screen and the men chasing the dozens of dalmatians, he spoke by rote. "Don't open the door for anyone but you or Aunt Laura."

So he was home again, Jack mused as he moved Roper into one of the stable stalls. Each time he'd come to the ranch or telephoned, he'd felt less anger. He and Sam had reached an understanding. They were congenial, though they would never be friends like before, and Jack would never work side by side with him or live on this ranch in the barn he'd called home. At eighteen, wanting independence, he'd moved into the original barn. The building had undergone enough changes to make it a home and for the next two weeks he'd lived there again.

After giving the horse feed, he turned to leave. Even in the shadowed light, he could see Sam waiting just inside, by the opened doors.

"Abby said you were here." With Jack's approach, the older man went on, "I'm glad you're home." His eyes narrowed to slits as if trying to see something more clearly. "We were beginning to worry. Roads get impassable during storms."

Abby. His mind still hung on the image of her, those dark eyes lacking the sparkle he'd remembered in them years ago. "I left Ogden later than I'd planned."

"Did you win?"

Jack nodded and moved closer to view the rain plummeting onto the dirt. "It was a small rodeo."

A frown suddenly crinkled deeper lines into Sam's tanned, weathered face. "I wanted you to know that I'm glad you could come home." He started to touch Jack's shoulder, then stopped himself. Instead, he dropped his arm to his side and tucked his hand in his pants pocket.

Jack squinted as much at him as against the wind blowing rain at his face. A polite way of saying, I'm glad you didn't refuse. "You're getting married. I'd be a lousy excuse for a son if I didn't come home for the wedding."

His father's head bobbed. "You'll like Laura."

Jack didn't doubt that. He recalled Abby talking about her aunt with warm affection.

"I'll never know what she sees in me," Sam said, "but she's told me that she's crazy about me." When he talked about Laura, he carried an air of joy, as if he'd won a lottery, one that had nothing to do with money. He was a man in love. Sixty-one years old and glowing from love. "I know rodeo life keeps you on the go. You've been busy with endorsements and public appearances. You said you did a television commercial, didn't you?"

Quit trying so hard, Sam, Jack wanted to say. "Yeah. For jeans." World champions were in demand. Next year, if he lost the title to someone else, no one would care what he was wearing. Jack gave him a token smile and deliberately shifted conversation away from himself. "You said business is good."

The ranch catered to city slickers intent on experiencing life on a ranch without losing the creature comforts of a four-star establishment complete with a swimming pool, tennis court, golf course and room service. But the Double M remained a working ranch, as well, with several hundred cattle, an ornery bull named Duncan and a stable of horses.

"The ranch keeps me too busy." Sam removed his Stetson and ran fingers through his cropped hair. "I could use help."

It was an indirect way of asking Jack to stay. Sam would never ask him outright to retire from rodeo.

Appearing embarrassed by his own words, Sam shrugged. "I'll see you at the lodge."

Maybe it would always be like this, Jack mused. Conversations filled with tension, words being carefully chosen, a lack of affection. He knew nothing would ever be the same.

With Abby, either, he reflected. Sam was responsible for that, too. If it hadn't been for Sam, he and Abby would be together.

Oh, hell, that wasn't true. He would never have been with her. He'd been footloose, chasing a dream. He wasn't sure she'd have wanted the life he was offering. But if it hadn't been for Sam, he wouldn't have left her that night, and he wouldn't have hurt her.

Abby stepped outside to the chill of the evening air but no rain. She shrugged into her windbreaker on the way to the car, and scanned the darkness.

Beyond the stables stood Sam's two-story, white farmhouse where her aunt was staying. Lights shone in several of its windows and in those at the ranch foreman's cottage. But unlike Sam's and Ray Guerny's homes, the renovated barn nearby that was Jack's home was dark.

In the distance, a coyote howled. When she'd left years ago, she never thought she'd be back, would hear that sound again. She still found it ironic that she'd lost love with one McShane male, but her aunt had found it with another.

At the car, she bent over and searched beneath

the pillow and blanket in the back seat. She found Austin's pack of bubble gum and a sketching toy. Wedged between the seat was a candy wrapper. Gathering the trash, she spotted the comic books under the front seat. Neatness wasn't her son's strongest trait.

She relocked the car door, then headed back toward the lodge. She'd always been a clean freak, even as a little girl. But then, her possessions had been few. Most of her childhood, she'd lived out of a suitcase. That life-style hadn't allowed for much clutter.

"It's been a long time, Abby."

She jerked to a stop, her heartbeat quickening. As she slowly faced him, Jack stepped out of the shadows. He was close enough to reach out, to touch her.

"You're looking good."

It's over. Mentally she said the words like a mantra. This chapter in your life closed long ago, she reminded herself. "Thank you. How are you?"

"I wasn't sure if you'd talk to me." Jack studied her. That was the truth. Leaving her as he had had been inexcusable. Though nearly a decade had passed, he'd been prepared for her bitterness when they met again.

Before leaving Boston, Abby had vowed that he'd never know how hurt she'd been. "That was eight years ago. I heard you're a celebrity now." How often had he told her that he was going to be a world champion? "You got what you wanted."

He'd wanted her. And he'd wanted rodeo. Logic had told him that he couldn't have both. "I guess." He'd been so tired earlier. He'd been driving since seven that morning from just the other side of the Utah border. When the rain had begun, he'd considered stopping somewhere for the night, but he'd been pulling the horse trailer, and he'd known that Roper would rest easier in a stable stall, so he'd kept going. Now he was glad he had. The tiredness had lifted because of her. He stuck a hand in his jeans pocket to keep from touching one of the soft silky strands framing her heart-shaped face. "The boy in the car—"

Abby raised her chin. "He's my son." *Our son.* Years ago, she'd buried her secret with long-distance phone calls to a ranch co-worker. Abby had fed her information about another man, needing the phantom lover to explain her pregnancy so no one at the ranch would guess the truth—would know she was pregnant with Jack's baby.

Earlier, when Jack had been moving Roper from the trailer to a stall, he'd watched her hug her aunt, noticed the boy, dark-haired, slim and tall like Abby. "What's his name?"

"Austin," Abby answered.

Several weeks after they'd gone their separate ways, he'd heard gossip that she'd already found another guy. Pride had demanded he not give a damn that she'd gotten over him so easily. But it had hurt. A lot.

He'd been told by Sam that there wasn't a husband. He guessed the boy's father had promised all she wanted, then let her down, too.

"I have to go back in." That wasn't a lie. She'd been gone from Austin longer than she felt comfortable with.

As shadows danced across her face, he couldn't stop himself from saying what he was thinking. "You look beautiful." An understatement, he mused. Reed-slim, she was dressed in snug-fitting jeans and a pale green T-shirt. She'd cut her reddish, straight hair to a shorter style that still brushed her shoulders but curved in layers toward her face. He stared into the darkness of her brown eyes, remembered them hooded, warm with passion. "I guess we'll have plenty of time to talk. You'll be here, what? Two weeks?"

"About that long. I should go, Jack." Abby climbed one step. Two people, once intimate, couldn't pretend to be only acquaintances, could they?

"Abby?"

He held her still with a word. In a small show of nerves, she lost her grip on her car keys. Breathe, she told herself, desperately trying to relax as she faced him.

Jack closed the distance between them, then bent over for the keys she'd just dropped. He smelled her perfume, a faint springy scent, a fragrance she'd always worn. Earlier, when he'd stood beside her car, he'd gotten a whiff of her perfume through the cracked window. In an instant, a memory of her dabbing several drops at the base of her neck had flashed back at him. "Here."

She looked down as he pressed her car keys into her hand. "Thank you."

"I'm glad to see you again," he said, and meant it. Of all the things he'd done in his life, he'd regretted most the way he'd left her.

What could she say? He smiled and she felt a twinge of panic because the young girl, the one who loved him, seemed so near. She stared a moment longer at the soft blue eyes, eyes that warmed her with a look, then she turned around and climbed the steps, not looking back. Years ago, she'd loved him, and he'd left her. With their son's comic books rolled and tightly gripped in her hand, she vowed not to forget that.

Chapter Two

Sound was everywhere. Birds chirped in the huge oaks, a rooster crowed, though it was past daybreak, a young colt whinnied as it pranced around the corral. The sounds of a ranch. Comforting, familiar sounds that Jack never tired of. He loved the land before him. He scanned the wide-open rangeland. Beyond the ranch buildings, desert vegetation of straggly-looking pale green bushes and a few cacti blended with distant hills.

He'd taken a morning ride to connect with the land again. As he neared the stable, Jack slowed his brown quarter horse, Roper. He'd won more than one championship on the animal. By the corral, he dismounted and stopped to watch a ranch hand clinging to the reins of a bucking mustang. Nearby, men perched on the railings of the corral and yelled encouraging words to him.

"Remember when you used to do that?"

Jack angled a look at Guy Guerny. "You, too." Because Ray, Guy's uncle, had been ranch foreman for nearly thirty-five years, the Guernys had always seemed to be part of Jack's life and of the ranch. Before, Ray's wife Lili was the ranch cook, now Guy's wife, Wendy, was.

Guy, a pal of Jack's since fourth grade, had shared the joy and often the consequences of youthful mischievous acts. They grew into manhood together, and for the past decade, they'd traveled the rodeo circuit.

"Yep." Guy hooked a thumb in the front pocket of his Levi's. "Seems like long ago."

Beside Jack, his horse nuzzled his long nose near Jack's arm as he looked for the treat in his pocket. "Just wait," he said on a laugh. "I'll give it to you after your saddle's off."

"Sometimes I think you're crazy. You and Mr. Ed," Guy quipped.

Jack stroked the long nose with its white patch. "He's insulting you, Roper, old boy. You're smarter than Mr. Ed, aren't you?" As if on cue, Roper snorted.

Guy sent him a wry grin that faded swiftly. "I saw Abby. Have you talked to her?"

"Last night." Jack had told his friend long ago why he'd needed to get away from the ranch, from Sam, even from Abby's sweetness. Too much anger had been churning within him. He hadn't been thinking straight that night eight years ago. He'd been blind with anger. And all the love Abby would have offered couldn't have reached him.

The next morning he'd awakened in his truck in a small town south of Los Angeles. His mood had gentled enough for him to talk to Abby, but by then it had been too late. He'd learned that she'd left the ranch. He'd decided then that he hadn't been offering what she'd longed for most. Sure, she'd nodded agreeably when he'd said no strings, but he'd never doubted that she really wanted the gold ring, kids and the white picket fence. So he'd done the right thing. He'd stayed away, aware she needed a man in her life who wanted to settle down. He hadn't been—still wasn't—that man.

Sunlight bathed the lobby and public rooms in a warm yellow glow. At ten-thirty in the morning, most of the tables were empty in the rustic dining room with its dark beams and wooden walls. Abby sat with Austin near one of the floor-to-ceiling windows. They offered a view of the distant mountains, the horse trail and the stream that ran through the property.

"Do you want more to eat?" she asked him as a waitress rounded their table and set a creamer before Abby.

Austin downed a glass of orange juice, then shook his head. "Can I go now?" Since he'd awakened, he'd been antsy for the day to start.

He'd barely touched his bowl of cereal, but Abby wasn't going to push him. No doubt he would get hungry long before lunch. Tomorrow morning some of his excitement would have settled, and he would eat breakfast as usual. Today, his exhilaration about everything new had stolen his appetite. Abby understood, so didn't play mother and nag. One day without breakfast wouldn't harm him.

''Mom?'' Austin's voice sang with impatience, indicating he'd been trying to get her attention during her reverie.

She leaned close and ran a fingertip down his nose. She hoped the day proved as wonderful as he was imagining. ''Yes, you can go.''

He bounced from the chair, sending it rocking. Quickly he straightened it, then shot her a grin. ''See you later, Mom.''

''I'll meet you back here at one-thirty for lunch.''

He flashed her a smile, and for one second, she saw Jack in that smile. ''I'll be here.'' He swung around and nearly plowed into a man.

Abby didn't need to see the man's face. It occurred to her how well she knew the look of Jack McShane from the belt buckle down.

''Hi.'' Austin raised his eyes to him.

During that second, Abby stopped breathing. Wasn't this moment why she'd really been dreading the return to the ranch? Here's your son, she wanted to say to him. But he wouldn't want to hear those words. He'd never lied to her. From the beginning of their relationship, he'd told her he wanted no ties.

In retrospect, she accepted that, when he'd left that night and she'd felt as if she would die from heartache without him, it hadn't been his fault. It had been her own. She'd actually believed that since she loved him, he would love her back. She'd been naive, foolish. She'd been like her mother, believing if she wished something to be true then it would be.

"You're Austin?" Jack asked.

Could he see himself in their son? Most people claimed Austin looked like her. He had her coloring, the same dark eyes, the thin nose. But she also saw Jack in him, in the smile, the shape of his face, the high cheekbones, the hint of handsomeness that would one day develop from his boyish good looks.

Clearly at a loss about a stranger knowing his name, Austin cast a troubled, puzzled expression back at her.

"This is Sam's son, Jack McShane," Abby told Austin. "Remember, he stopped his truck last night for us."

"It was spooky."

Jack grinned at the child. He had eyes like Abby, warm and expressive.

How could Jack look at Austin and not see? Abby wondered. She supposed that was silly thinking. But she sensed she would know Austin was hers even if she met him suddenly after years of separation.

Jack offered his hand to the boy. "It's nice to meet you, Austin."

With that handshake, Abby knew he'd won Austin's favor by treating him like a grown-up. Her heart twisted at the sight of Austin's small boy's hand enveloped by his father's large, callused one. Blood of my blood, flesh of my flesh.

"Mom said you're a rodeo champion. That's really neat, Mr. McShane."

"Call me Jack."

A pleased expression broadened his youthful grin. "Thanks. Got to go." He darted a look at Abby for approval. "Okay?"

"Yes, it's okay."

In a flurry of motion, he scurried around Jack and dashed across the gleaming hardwood floor toward the door.

"One-thirty," Abby called out as a reminder. Her words hung in the air. Austin was already out the door.

"What was his hurry?" Jack asked.

He really looked wonderful, Abby thought, discreetly taking in his well-broken-in and well-scuffed cowboy boots. Dust-shrouded jeans clung to his lean hips and followed the hard contours of long legs. A plain leather belt with a large silver buckle held his blue work shirt in place.

"Before coming to breakfast, I signed him up for the supervised activities." She'd also secured the name of an employee to babysit in case she wanted an evening to herself. "They're having the kids pan for gold today," she told him. Under the supervised care, the children could learn not only about Native lore, rocks and crafts, but also how to swim and horseback-ride.

"Sounds as if he's settling in. What about you?"

Nervous, Abby drew a deep breath while he pulled out a chair across the table from her. "It's nice to be back."

"Still inhale caffeine?" he asked, noting she'd poured another cup from the carafe on the table between them. She used to consume a day's worth of coffee before nine.

"I do better now." She turned the humor on herself. "I eat a token breakfast of toast. To set a good example."

He matched her smile. He knew it was dumb, but he was having a devil of a time remembering she was a mother. She looked as fresh-faced and young as she had the last time he'd seen her.

Abby raised her gaze to Sam who had come into the dining hall and now stood beside their table.

"Morning." He smiled at her, but his words were for Jack. "I forgot to mention earlier that there's a ranchers' meeting here next week."

Jack said nothing. Getting involved in ranch business didn't interest him. He wouldn't stay, not ever.

"If you come, it would give you a chance to see everyone again before the wedding," Sam reminded him.

Sam McShane had never bowed to anyone. It gave Jack no pleasure that his father was tiptoeing around him. What he hadn't said but what had come through clearly was that neighbors and friends would expect him to be there. In their minds, the Double M was his ranch, too. "I'll be there." For appearance's sake, to save Sam from embarrassment, he'd do what was necessary. What he'd never do is forget what his father had done.

"Fine." Sam delivered another smile before leaving them, but Abby had noticed the look of relief that had swept over his face. What had happened between this father and son? she wondered.

"Do you want the blueberry or apple pie?" a server was asking Jack.

"Blueberry."

Abby knew that he was an early riser no matter what time he went to bed. At daybreak, he'd probably had a full breakfast. "Who's the new cook?" she asked when they were alone.

"Wendy."

"Really?" Abby had worked side by side with her, waiting on tables. She'd been a freckled-face waitress with a winsome smile who'd had a terrific crush on Guy. She'd also been the never-give-up type.

"She's Guy's wife now. She supervises the meals that come from the kitchen to the dining room. An old-timer named Dugan handles the cooking chores for the ranch hands."

"She and Guy married?" Abby remembered the lean wrangler with the quick grin, a buddy of Jack's. Guy had seemed just as unwilling as Jack to settle down. Back then, he'd humored the girl who'd been several years younger than him. "Wendy was tenacious," she said.

"Guy learned that. They got married about four

years ago." He, too, liked the petite blonde with her wholesome good looks. They'd become friends quickly, probably because they had something in common; they both cared about Guy. "They had a little girl last year."

As he looked up from the pie and chuckled, Abby traced his stare to a bright-faced blonde who'd just come through the kitchen's swinging door. "Wendy!" Abby was already standing, rushing toward her for a hug. "Oh, you don't look any different."

Wendy pulled back but held on to Abby's hands. "You, either. I could hardly believe it when Guy told me you were here, that Laura was your aunt. She's just great. We all really like her."

Abby was glad to hear that her aunt was being welcomed by so many people who were important to the ranch. "I heard you're a mommy."

While beaming at her, Wendy ran a dust-floured hand down the front of the white apron covering her jeans. "You, too."

"Yes, me, too."

"I wish I could stay and talk, but—" Wendy pulled a face. "I have to go back in the kitchen. We'll have to get together again. I want you to meet Jodi."

"Your little girl?"

"She's beautiful," she said unabashedly.

Just being with Wendy made her feel twenty-one again. "And you can meet Austin."

Wendy laid a hand on Abby's shoulder and patted

it gently. "Your son's one step ahead of you. I've already met him."

"You have? When? We've only been here since late last night."

"He needed a doughnut at six this morning. He came into the kitchen, clutching his stomach and insisting he would faint without one."

Abby rolled her eyes. No wonder he wasn't hungry at breakfast this morning. "He's going to be an actor."

Wendy laughed and stepped back. "Later."

"Yes." Abby settled on her chair again and turned to Jack. "It's wonderful seeing her. Are any of the others who used to work here still around?"

Relaxing, Jack stretched out long, denim-clad legs under the table. "A few. But there are a lot of new faces. When I called Sam a few weeks ago, he complained about the turnaround. Some of them hire on, then can't hack the heat in summer, or the bugs, or the dust. You know."

Abby couldn't help smiling. Having lived all her life in a city, when she'd come to the Double M eight years ago, she'd been one of those people who'd needed a period of adjustment.

"What about your aunt? Do you really think she's going to be happy here?"

His question bothered her. "Why not?"

"I don't know." Hunched forward, he took a hearty bite of pie. "Run it by me again. Sam met your aunt through you? Is that right?" he asked.

"At a horse auction in Texas. Aunt Laura lives

there. Austin and I were visiting her. I saw Sam at the auction and introduced him to Laura. Eight months later—here we are.''

Jack sort of smiled. ''She has horses?'' He'd gotten the impression that Laura was more comfortable on the cushy seat of a luxury car than on a saddle.

''No, she doesn't. But she likes them.''

Jack's doubts strengthened. His father and Abby's aunt sounded ill suited for each other. He remembered when Abby had first come to the ranch. She'd moaned about missing her once-a-week-outing at the movies, her nightly walk to the coffee shop, her Saturday mornings window-shopping.

She'd liked everything Jack hadn't. He'd liked everything she hadn't. She wouldn't touch a steak, his favorite. He wouldn't stick a fork in a rice bowl of her favorite, teriyaki chicken, much less use chopsticks. He never drank coffee, rarely went to the movies, thought shopping a waste of time. She had no idea how to two-step, couldn't stomach jalapeño peppers and had never been on a horse.

But he'd been crazy about her.

Before the summer had ended, she was horse-back-riding, he was drinking coffee with her and they were two-stepping at the local hangout.

Abby lifted her eyes from her coffee cup. ''Was that all you wanted to know?''

Jack cut short more reminiscing thoughts. ''What does Laura do?''

After one last stir, Abby removed her spoon from her cup. ''Do?''

It occurred to Jack that Sam might be viewing life through an infatuated haze. "Work. What kind of work does she do?"

"She owns a boutique in Houston that she plans to sell."

Even the way she lived contradicted Sam's. This was none of his business. What Sam did stopped mattering to him years ago, but… No buts, he berated himself.

"You don't like my aunt?" She asked the question, but had a hard time believing it. Her aunt was a people person. She had a mild temper, rarely ever getting angry. She liked yellow roses and old Rodgers and Hammerstein musicals. She liked spinach enchiladas. And she liked people who appreciated what they had in life.

"I like her," he replied. That was the truth. Laura was easy to talk to, lovely, almost sweet.

Abby sipped the last of her coffee. "You have doubts about them, don't you? You think this is a mistake."

"What I think doesn't matter."

Why didn't it? she wondered. Why had he distanced himself from his father? She remembered when Sam and Jack had been as much friends as father and son. Perhaps because he'd started the conversation, she allowed her own misgivings to surface. "My aunt does seem blindly euphoric," she admitted.

Abby looked out the window at the desert. Would her aunt be happy living way out here? It might be fun for a vacation, but what about day in and day out for the rest of her life? "Instead of considering how different her life will be when she marries and lives here, her biggest concern is how many tiers to make the wedding cake."

"What's that chicken dish called that she wants Wendy to make?" he asked, remembering a conversation he overheard between Sam and Wendy early this morning.

Abby brought her gaze back to him. "Chicken Kiev." A frown settled on her face. Painfully, Abby began listing differences. "Laura stays up late. Sam goes to bed early, doesn't he?"

"At ten."

"Laura's on her way out the door at that time." Abby had called her aunt often enough after putting Austin to bed to learn that her aunt was leaving for a gallery opening or party.

As a small frown line formed between her eyebrows, Jack thought she looked adorable. "A night of fun to Sam is having a barbecue at a neighbor's."

"That's good though." She sounded hopeful. "My aunt loves parties."

Jack couldn't help being skeptical. Not all parties were the same. "In some penthouse apartment. Not outside with the dust and bugs and paper plates."

He made her laugh with his exaggeration, but then, he always could. "I know for a fact it isn't that unpleasant."

He wanted to keep the moment light. "They don't sound like a match made in heaven, do they?"

Abby heard more tease than criticism in his voice. "I'd like to believe it won't hurt them that they're so different. Sometimes opposites attract."

"Sometimes."

The softness in his voice made her look up. He'd moved his hand, hadn't he? Yes, she decided. It was definitely closer. Her eyes locked on his. How easy it was to be with him. But this time she wouldn't let heat fog her mind. They'd been so different. He'd thrived on thrills, new places, new faces. She hadn't wanted to flutter like a butterfly from one place to another. She'd wanted stability, a house of her own, a place to let roots grab hold.

Was she remembering all the differences? Jack wondered. With movement nearby, he looked away. "Here's someone else you know," he said to her.

Curious, Abby swiveled a look over her shoulder and saw another face from the past. "Ray." She bolted to a stand as the ranch foreman came close. He'd been Sam's right-hand man for thirty-five years. Guy's uncle looked tired. He also looked enchanted with the toddler in his arms, Abby thought.

"Well, look at you." Grinning, he scratched at his gray beard, then curled one arm around Abby's shoulder to draw her close for a hug.

"It's wonderful to see you, Ray."

"This is Guy and Wendy's little one. Jodi."

"It's nice to meet you, too," Abby said, touching one of Jodi's chubby cheeks.

"She's a real scooter," Ray said proudly about his grand-niece.

Abby ran a hand over the little one's soft dark hair. "And the apple of your eye."

Jodi pushed her small, stuffed teddy bear at Abby.

Jack laughed, and standing now, opened his arms to her. "She thinks everyone should want that motley thing."

Ray transferred the child to Jack. "Gonna walk with me and see that colt?"

"Might as well." He skimmed Abby's hand, then stepped away.

She struggled for a smile. Pain, physical pain, swelled in her chest as she stared after him with Guy and Wendy's child in his arms. In self-defense, she rushed a reminder. What happened hadn't been entirely her fault. She'd have told him about the baby if he hadn't left so suddenly.

Abby drew in several long, deep breaths as the memory of that last night closed in on her. She'd been stunned when she learned he'd left. She'd walked away, numb.

When she'd reached her room, she'd wept. For him. For herself. For what she wanted and couldn't allow herself to have with him. And for their baby inside her.

For too many months after leaving Arizona, she'd thought about Jack. Too many times, she'd nearly called the ranch to get news about him. Too often, she'd searched newspapers for his name among the winners at some rodeo.

Then, as their child had grown within her, she'd made herself face reality, and had stopped wishful thinking. Motherhood had forced her to give up dreaming. She'd had a child to think about, to be responsible for. Since then, for eight years, she'd made a life for her and Austin without Jack. Two weeks with him now would change nothing.

Chapter Three

Three days passed, and Abby couldn't shake a feeling of discontent. She spent another afternoon basking in the sun poolside. But the lounging around made her edgy. She blamed the mood on idleness. She wasn't used to so much time for herself. She was a working single mother. She loved her job at the newspaper, writing special interest stories, but her life was usually hectic.

Dressed, not knowing what else to do, she strolled along the path at the back of the lodge that led to a pavilion and rows of picnic tables where a western barbecue for tourists would take place on Saturday night.

She supposed part of the problem was Jack. Of course, she was uneasy being around him again.

She'd felt a twinge of old feelings when she'd been with him earlier and that bothered her. For years, good sense had led her, then the moment he came into her life again, showed her a little attention, she was that young girl once more. And seeing him with a child in his arms had been unnerving.

Annoyed with herself, she began to walk back to the lodge. It was silly to start doubting herself now about the decision she'd made almost a decade ago. She'd done the right thing. She and Austin needed a man who would always be there for them, a for-ever kind of man. That wasn't Jack. It would never be Jack.

Nearing the playground area, she caught a glimpse of her son climbing over a corral fence with one of his friends.

"Mom! Hi, Mom." His face slightly sunburned from an afternoon beneath the Arizona sun, he bar-reled toward her while his buddy ran up the lodge steps.

Austin deserved more than Jack would offer. Long ago he'd declared "no marriage, no kids." He didn't want to be a father, she reminded herself for good measure.

"I came in second in the go-cart race," Austin said.

Abby smiled at him. "That's great."

He delivered a hug, then went on excitedly. "An older boy won it, but I had lots of fun."

She'd taught him that, she reflected, pleased that he understood he wouldn't always be a winner.

What mattered most was that he did his best, that he had fun. As a single mother, she'd fretted about carrying the roles of mother and father. Eventually she'd resigned herself with the same advice she'd given her son. All she could do was her best.

Austin continued to chatter while they ambled inside the lodge. "Then we had a water fight with squirt bottles."

She'd guessed some similar activity—her blouse was damp from being pressed against his soaked T-shirt. Before they left Boston, she'd never doubted that he would have fun while he was at the ranch. She'd remembered her own joy here, once she'd adjusted to her new environment. How could a person wake to the fresh country air, hear a rooster, ride a horse beneath a summer's sun, and not feel a connection with the land? Some of the most wonderful days of her life had been here.

"And Jack said it was all right with him."

Those words snapped her attention back to the boy. "What did Jack say was all right? When did you see him?"

"Mom, you're frowning again."

"Austin, I thought you were in a go-cart race."

"I was." He answered her but looked elsewhere, distracted by a boy a year or two older and his parents who stood before the registration desk. Curiosity laced his voice. "Are they coming or going, Mom?"

"Coming." Abby reached for patience. She had to remember that he wouldn't understand why she placed so much importance on any meeting he had with Jack. "Austin, where did you see Jack?"

"In the stables."

When? "What were you doing in the stables?" She wanted to give him freedom to enjoy the sights and sounds of the ranch, but she couldn't have him wandering around without her knowing where he was.

His eyes went wide with worry. "Am I in trouble? Did I do something wrong?"

"Did you tell me you were going there?"

"I thought it was all right. I went with the other kids after the go-cart race. Guy took us there."

Aware that Guy was helping with the kids, Abby mentally grimaced. "Austin, I'm sorry," she said about jumping to conclusions. "I thought you went by yourself."

An expression of bewilderment bunched his eyebrows. "That's one of the rules, isn't it? I'm not supposed to go somewhere without telling you or Aunt Laura."

Abby touched the top of his head. He was a good boy. "So you saw Jack." It hadn't been a meeting of only the two of them, she knew now.

"He used a—a pick to clean dirt from the horse's hoof. He said it would be all right for me to try doing it sometime."

She wasn't so sure she wanted her son that close to a horse's hoof.

"He's a real cowboy, Mom. Did you know that?"

"Yes, I know," she answered, not unaware of how impressed Austin was.

"There's Nicki." Austin pointed at a little girl, a guest, he'd met yesterday.

Abby had talked to the girl's parents, made sure they didn't view her son joining them as an intrusion on their family fun. She'd thought of suggesting a hike together, but she guessed his eagerness to be with his new friend. "Go ahead and play."

As he dashed off, calling the girl's name, Abby looked around her. Now what? This was impossible, she decided. She wasn't used to so much free time. She needed something to do or she'd go crazy for the next two weeks. Surely Sam and her aunt could use help with the wedding plans.

On the way to Sam's office, she snagged a magazine from the rack in the lobby. She saw the office door was open and stepped near, but voices stopped her at the threshold. Wendy was talking nonstop, not to Sam, but to Jack. Perched on the edge of the desk, he looked her way, pinned her with smiling eyes.

"She called and said she's been arrested," Wendy was telling him. "Sunbeam—"

"Sunbeam is an assistant cook," Jack said, offering Abby information that drew her in to their conversation.

Wendy rolled her eyes. "That's the name she wants to be called by this month."

Amused, Jack grinned wryly. He'd entered the office to get the keys for a shed, and Wendy had cornered him with her problem. "Did you tell Sam that his assistant cook is in jail for growing something other than basil on her windowsill?''

Exasperation threaded Wendy's voice. ''That's what I'm telling you. I can't find him to tell him, and I can't wait around. What if he doesn't come back until evening? We'll have wasted a full day. We have to put out the word that we're short of help and get a replacement.''

''You can manage without her, can't you? Being short one employee won't shut down the lodge,'' he said as he placed a calming hand on Wendy's shoulder.

''I don't have a problem with today. But we have the Saturday-night barbecue for tourists and then the ranchers' meeting. I'll need help cooking. She was my assistant, Jack. You know everyone has specific jobs. One person missing will cause problems that night and I can't train someone new in a few days to know the kitchen, know where to find supplies, what to do, and— Oh, Abby,'' Wendy said as she caught sight of her in the doorway. A speculative tone brightened her voice. A light came into her eyes. ''Abby, would you…?''

Abby was already nodding in response to the unasked question.

''You'll do it?'' Wendy left Jack's side to close the distance to her.

''Until you get someone.'' She was grateful to have something to do. ''It'll be like old times.''

''What have they talked you into?'' Sam asked from the doorway.

"Oh, Sam, you're back." Wendy looked jubilant. Quickly she filled him in on her dilemma. "And Abby's volunteered to help for the next few days, so I won't be short help for the weekend barbecue."

Sam's troubled gaze angled toward Abby. "We couldn't ask you to do this."

She saw no problem. "I don't need training." Since arriving, she'd written off her discontent as nerves about seeing Jack, but that was only part of the problem. She'd been feeling out-of-step with her surroundings, because she wasn't comfortable with the idea of sitting around as a guest. "I know how to make the recipes. Remember?"

Laughing, Sam held his hands in the air. "I believe you." Affection slipped into his voice. "You are a lifesaver. But what will your aunt say?"

Abby thought it sweet that he was so concerned about Laura's opinion. "If she knew what to do, she would help."

Sam broke into a smile. "You're right, of course. She's a good sport. And not afraid of hard work."

"Good," Wendy was saying as she began walking away. "That's settled then. Come to the kitchen when you're ready," she called back to Abby.

"You really don't mind?" Sam questioned one more time.

Abby's only concern was the time she would spend away from Austin during the next two days. But with the friends he'd met and all the activities available, she knew he would be busy. "Really," she assured Sam.

In a brief all-too-familiar gesture, Jack's fingertips caressed her waist before he passed her and Sam and left the room.

Sam returned a semblance of a broad grin, but a disturbance lingered in his eyes. "I'm sure sorry you two aren't still together," he said when Jack was gone.

Abby managed a weak smile. She could hardly say, He left. I was pregnant, so I left.

Sam's expression turned wistful. "I really thought you were going to stay in his life. But I guess you did all right with someone else. That's a fine boy you have."

"Thank you, Sam." Abby averted her gaze. The rippling effect of her deception suddenly occurred to her. Like Jack, Sam had been cheated of years with Austin. As Sam's phone rang, she took a step back and toward the door. "Bye."

Her own guilt shadowed her while she ambled into the kitchen to help Wendy. Though Jack had wanted no part of fatherhood, Sam would have welcomed being called grandpa, and she'd taken that from him.

For hours Abby helped one of the kitchen staff. They counted tin plates, rolled silverware in napkins and lined up plastic glassware for the following evening's barbecue. It was a night for over two hundred tourists that offered a quickly served western dinner, country music and silly skits under the stars. Abby had always enjoyed the fun weekly barbecue, even as a worker.

At six that evening, she stopped working to have dinner with Austin, then returned to the kitchen. Later, she left again to get him settled in bed. In his room, while he undressed, he told her about the boy who'd just arrived.

"Chris and me and Jack played baseball after dinner."

Sitting on the edge of his bed, Abby handed him his pajama top. "Did you?"

He yanked the top of his Captain Cosmo pajamas over his head. "Jack can hit a ball far, Mom," he said in a muffled voice. His head popped through the opening. "He's real good at lots of stuff."

Abby knew that too well. She summoned up a smile, but troubled thoughts stayed with her. She waited until he fell asleep and the baby-sitter had arrived, then returned to the kitchen. She'd never considered the possibility that Jack would show such interest in Austin.

"Hello, sweetheart," her aunt said breezily when Abby pushed open the kitchen's swinging door.

Abby nearly misstepped at the sight of her aunt standing at one of the counters, dicing celery. "You're helping?"

"I'm not totally inept in the kitchen." Laura made a face. "Although I do make pancakes that resemble Frisbees," she told Wendy who was cutting watermelon into bite-size pieces. "Sam is in his office compiling information for the ranchers' meeting, so I thought I'd do something useful.''

''Glad to have the help,'' Wendy said.

''She's a lovely girl,'' Laura said when Wendy went to the cellar. ''In fact, everyone is so nice.'' She set down the knife. ''I was nervous about meeting Jack.''

Abby hefted a bag of potatoes onto the table. ''Why?'' she asked while retrieving a potato peeler from a drawer.

Laura had resumed chopping. ''Sam hasn't been serious about anyone since his wife died.''

''Aunt Laura, Jack never knew his mother. She died when he was born.'' Abby dug into the potato sack. His mother had died and he'd carried the burden of that for the rest of his life. Abby always wondered how different everything would have been between them if she'd lived. ''I never want to risk some woman's life to have my child,'' Jack had told her one night.

''I heard that,'' her aunt replied, ''but he might have some image of a woman who is larger than life.''

Abby leaned over the table toward Laura, and squeezed her hand. ''Someone just like you.''

Laura's laughter rippled out. ''You, my dear, are silly. But I don't need to worry. Jack has been so wonderful.''

Abby had thought the same thing about him for months one summer.

''Here you are.''

Abby silently groaned as Wendy entered the kitchen and hauled in a second sack of potatoes.

For the next few hours, the three women passed time telling stories, drinking coffee and munching on cookies while peeling and cutting potatoes.

Though Laura left at eleven-thirty, Abby kneaded dough for biscuits for a while longer.

Yawning, Wendy stood and stretched. "Enough," she insisted and nudged Abby toward the door. "Tomorrow we'll do the rest. Go to bed."

Abby wasn't ready for sleep. Needing to unwind, she wandered outside. A drizzle had begun. She'd always liked walking in the rain, liked the excitement of sound that came from the pelting rain. She liked the way the sky lit up as if a celebration was taking place.

In the distance, lightning streaked across the sky. A downpour began, fat raindrops plopping on her. Abby scrunched her shoulders and darted toward the barn to take shelter until the storm passed. As the sky burst with light, she stepped into the barn.

"You once told me it took your breath away."

Abby jolted, her head snapping up. A hand to her chest, she felt her heart's fast beat.

Perched on a bale of hay only feet from her, Jack smiled slowly. "Sorry. I didn't mean to scare you."

His hair, glossy and darker from the moisture, was slicked back, his face was beaded by raindrops. Unexpectedly she felt a longing to press her hands against the wetness of his lean cheeks.

"Only you would be out in this weather," he teased.

Was that lazy drawl of his what she'd fallen in love with first? She couldn't say now what had brought them together. Chemistry? Probably. "And you." His eyes met hers, and she felt swept back in time. Was the sight of the rain reminding him of moments when the headiness of lovemaking had enveloped them? What did it matter? she wondered. "I heard you spent time after dinner with Austin."

"Playing ball." To Jack's surprise, he'd enjoyed himself. The boy had rambled, told him about their life in Boston. They lived in a five-room apartment in a three-story brownstone with a neighbor above them who played the accordion. The boy liked school but not math. His mom made him cookies, his favorite snack, and when she had time, she baked cupcakes, too. Jack had listened, amused by the boy's stories about a bird he'd found hurt and had cared for, about the snowball he'd tried to save in a dresser drawer that had melted all over his socks. "He told me he has a dead scorpion in a jar," he said, sharing a story with her that had made him chuckle.

"He does," Abby said, aware he'd thought Austin was making up some tale. The desert souvenir was her son's subtle way of reminding her that he wanted a pet. She felt terrible that she couldn't give Austin the one thing he wanted most, a dog. "I'll be glad when his fascination with bugs and reptiles ends."

"I gathered he liked them. It's a phase," Jack said with certainty. "I was fascinated with them, too."

Lightning flashed again, casting the inside of the barn in a ghostly whiteness, illuminating his face in an eerie glow. "When did it end?"

"When I noticed that Michelle Adams didn't like them." She responded with a smile, but he noted that she looked sleepy, her eyes hooded. "Are you sorry you volunteered to help in the kitchen?"

Abby didn't hesitate. "No." She finally felt comfortable being at the ranch again. "I wanted to do something."

"You like peeling potatoes?"

"Actually, my aunt finished that." She noticed the surprise that flickered in his eyes at her aunt helping. "I'm the biscuit maker now." Out of the corner of her eye, she saw the ranch cat nervously stalking in the overhead loft as the wind wailed and whistled through the building. "I'd forgotten how much work goes into one of these evenings. My aunt asked when Sam had started these dinners for the tourists. Neither Wendy nor I could remember. Do you?"

Just one more time he'd like to be with her, he realized. "One summer about ten years ago, a busload of folks got stranded here. Sam organized the dinner for them, and it's grown bigger every year."

"If I remember right, a couple of hundred people come to it."

Lazily his gaze roamed over her face. "That sounds right."

The western-style barbecue with entertainment was profitable to other businesses in town, drawing in tourists. In fact, it had become a highlight of Saturday nights during the summer.

"Sam said you're working for a newspaper in Boston now."

Abby nodded. She saw no harm in the casual, let's-play-catch-up conversation. "I do special-interest articles." She'd spent years of hard work, of playing gofer, doing whatever to get a column. For a while, she'd written obituaries. "I was Dear Emily for a few months."

Her smile, a familiar one, appeared whiter in the dark interior of the barn. "Who's Dear Emily?"

"That's the advice columnist."

As amusement spread over her face in a way he'd seen dozens of times, Jack ached to grab her and draw her close. Nothing was over between them, he knew in that second. "I heard you won a press award for a story about day-care centers."

That he knew such a detail about her life surprised her. "Who told you?"

"Laura mentioned it."

"Oh." Abby could guess how that conversation had gone. "She went on forever about me, didn't she?"

Jack hadn't minded listening to Laura, learning what Abby had done with her life since leaving the ranch. "Why shouldn't she have bragging rights? You worked really hard." The serious young girl who'd told him once that she couldn't waste her education had done well.

Everything had been easier for him. He'd stopped rodeoing to go to agricultural college for two years, then had walked away from education for rodeo again. It had been in his blood.

But she'd worked, struggled for her education. She'd just turned twenty-one when she'd come to the ranch. Looking back, Jack realized how vulnerable she'd been. The month before that, her mother had been hit by a truck while walking home from work. Abby had told him that she'd reeled from the shock of her death and had grabbed at somewhere to go, to get away from their apartment. That was the *real* reason she'd taken the job at the ranch.

"Why so quiet?" A blast of wind tossed her hair back from her face, emphasizing her fragility.

"I never listen to the rain when I'm in the city," she said as an excuse. Looking up, she saw him bend his right leg slowly in an exercising motion, saw a trace of discomfort in his face. "Your father said you had an injury. What happened?"

"The bull was anxious to get out and sandwiched my knee between him and the chute. I've been out of commission for the past three months."

She knew him. He must have hated that inactivity.

"I'll bet Sam said lots more." That she kept silent forced him to go on. "He thinks I should stay. He thought I might have gotten rodeo fever out of my system when I had the injury."

"Why would he? Rodeo has always been part of your life."

He felt old suddenly. Sam knew what he didn't want to face. Too many injuries and he'd be sidelined for good. "Since I was away from it for a while, and out of the limelight, he probably figured I'd get used to a life that didn't include driving for two days to spend eight seconds on a bull."

She doubted his plan to return to rodeo was what had caused the tension between father and son, but she knew prying was hopeless. If Jack didn't want to talk about something, nothing changed his mind.

"It rained the night we met," he said. "Remember?"

Abby noticed he'd moved to view the rain, and found herself staring at his broad back. "I remember." She'd never forget any moment she'd had with him. She'd been in town after spending a couple of hours in the movie theater. Ray had spotted her walking through the parking lot to her car and had stopped for a moment to talk to her. He'd stood beside his truck, told her he'd come to town to pick up Guy, his nephew, and Sam's son from the airport.

For weeks, she'd listened to every single, female employee at the ranch gushing about both men, obviously smitten by their rodeo status. Abby had attempted to act indifferent, but she'd been curious about Guy and Jack.

Ray had asked her if she wanted to come along. Seated behind her steering wheel, Abby had refused, a touch nervous about meeting the rodeo Casanovas.

She'd been about to say goodbye to Ray when he'd broken out in a sweat and had clutched at his chest. She'd gotten help quickly, was told by the paramedics that Ray had had a heart attack before they'd pulled away to take him to the hospital.

Abby had driven to the airport to get Guy and Jack.

"You were so worried about Ray." Jack turned and moved near. "I remember the way you came up to Guy, touched him, told him the news about his uncle as gently as you could."

"I didn't want to panic him."

"I think you're the only reason he didn't. You were cool in a crisis." Was there any memory of her forgotten? "You always were."

She met his eyes steadily, even as she knew if she stared too long he could make her forget the hurt, weaken her. On that night, she'd driven Guy and Jack to the hospital. They'd waited with Guy until word had come that Ray was okay.

Later, rain had begun. Drops had dueled with the windshield wipers as she'd sat in the car with Jack and driven him to the ranch. Until that moment, she'd been too concerned for Ray to think about the man who, with a smile, buckled women's knees. Then Jack's eyes had locked with hers. In an instant, she'd known she was as lost to his riveting good looks as every admirer or groupie he'd attracted. The next morning he'd sat in the ranch dining room and smiled at her. From that moment on, they were inseparable.

Unable to resist, Jack touched a strand of her hair. It still felt like silk threads between his fingers. He knew that she had a right to want no part of him. He'd left her. But there had been a moment the next day when he'd thought they could still have a chance. A phone call to the ranch had told him differently. "Why did you leave here so quickly?"

She stared at him in disbelief. "Why did I? You left first." Frowning, she said, "Wait a minute. How do you know I left quickly?"

Was there any point in rehashing the past? "I called the next morning to talk to you."

Vulnerability suddenly riding high, Abby swayed back. "You called?" *He called.* What if…? Don't go there, she warned herself. She wanted to ask questions, but he'd moved closer. With his breath fluttering across her face, even thinking took effort. And all the what ifs in the world wouldn't change anything now.

"I wasn't leaving you, Abby." He spoke the truth. "I was leaving Sam. When I called, Lili told me you'd packed and left at eight that morning." Lightly he stroked a thumb across her wrist, then moved his fingers higher on her arm. In the slight muscle of her forearm, he felt her tense almost combatively. But beneath his spread fingers, he'd also felt her pulse scramble. "Did you ever wonder what might have been between us?"

She didn't need a man who would leave without a second thought. For Austin, she needed a stable man, one who was willing to accept the responsibilities of a family. Jack had made clear years ago he wasn't that man. "We wouldn't have lasted."

He dealt with a flash of annoyance. "So all that happened was for the best?"

"Probably."

An urge to prove her wrong strengthened.

"I still want what you don't," Abby said simply. "Roots, home, family."

To be with him, she'd pretended she didn't want any of that. But he knew her better than she realized. "Yes, I did always want that."

Jack studied her closely. In the darkness, her skin appeared pale. He leaned toward her and slipped his fingers through strands of her hair, then cupped the back of her head to draw her face a hairbreadth from his. "And I always wanted you."

His voice curled around her like a caress. Rain softly pattered against the ground. Overhead, thunder cracked as if determined to shake the buildings below it, while inside her a storm of a different kind brewed.

When he brushed a knuckle across her throat, she stopped breathing. She could have pulled back, moved away. But she didn't. She wanted to prove that it was over. So when his mouth slanted across hers, she parted her lips, accepted his kiss. In the next instant, she called herself a fool. Pleasure slithered through her, and all the years of yearning for his taste took over.

On a sigh, she closed her eyes while she savored the moment, memorized everything, from the gentleness of his arms on her back to the strength of his body against hers. Rain pelted against the roof as if keeping time with the cadence of her heart.

Molded to his body, she felt heat flow from him into her. She recognized the danger building within her, but she didn't pull away. She strained against him. Another sigh escaped from her throat as his breath warmed her mouth.

She wished he meant nothing to her. She wished she could walk away and not crave more. But the firm, warm lips on hers reminded her of the loneliness and aching that she'd felt since the last time she'd stood like this in his arms. Familiar sensations dissolved the years. She felt as if it was yesterday, when he filled her days with such happiness, when she was so in love she couldn't think straight. Lips clinging to his, she drifted back in time with him for another moment. Only a moment.

Yesterdays are over, a small voice in her brain nagged. And so were they. Before she couldn't, before all that was wrong between them was forgotten, she tore her mouth from his. "Please. It is over," she insisted more for herself than him, even as she wanted to fall back into his arms.

She didn't dare give him time to respond. Still breathless, she left the barn and rushed toward the lodge. With the rain pouring down on her, she laid a fingertip against her lips. They felt warm and swollen. He wanted only moment to moment with her, she tried to remember. She wanted more, deserved more. Austin deserved more.

Not until she reached the hallway to her room did she allow the emotion strangling her to grab hold. He was everything she'd ever wanted. It was a fact she'd been trying to deny for eight years.

At the door she stopped, closed her eyes and rested her forehead against it. Both familiar and new feelings, some she'd thought she'd buried eight years ago, engulfed her. She'd been so sure that when she saw him she would feel nothing.

She fought the tightening in her throat, the tears smarting her eyes. As her heart finally slowed to a normal pace, she wasn't certain what she felt for him would ever be over.

Chapter Four

With morning, Abby felt only annoyance that Jack could still tilt her world, still make her weak. She knew she was vulnerable to him, but she was also determined not to let one kiss and the feelings he stirred override good sense.

In the kitchen with Wendy, she rolled out dough for piecrust with more gusto than necessary. Until she left the ranch, she had to remember she never would have seen Jack again if her aunt wasn't marrying Sam.

Wondering about Austin in the dining room, she wiped her hands on a towel, then wandered out of the kitchen. She spotted him sitting at a window table with her aunt and Sam.

''We've been discussing fishing,'' her aunt informed Abby with her approach. She couldn't help noticing that Laura and Sam wore matching smiles.

Head bent, Austin dipped his spoon into a bowl of dinosaur-shaped cereal. "Sam is going to let me borrow his best lure."

Fishing had been on his mind before they left Boston. "That's nice."

"So it's okay if I go?"

"Go?" Abby realized they weren't discussing something he might do in the future.

"Jack said we could go fishing."

Uneasiness intensified within her. What was happening here?

"I told him that I'd never been fishing. He said that was the best reason to go." Austin looked absolutely thrilled. "So can I? You could go, too, Mom. Do you want to?"

Staring at the delight dancing in her son's eyes, she would have given him anything he'd asked for at that moment. "You can go."

"You, too, Mom? Will you go with us?"

They'd done so little together since arriving. "Did Jack say when?"

"Today. This afternoon," he said. "Or do you have to help Wendy?"

"We're almost done until later." She touched his arm. "But I have some finishing up to do." Assured he wasn't eating alone, she ambled back to the kitchen to finish the pies. As soon as she was done, she planned to find Jack. She needed to understand why he'd invited Austin to spend an afternoon with him.

Not for the first time, Wendy thanked her when she returned to the kitchen. "I promise I'll have someone hired before next weekend," she said while she set cans of blueberry-pie filling on the counter.

"Don't worry."

"I really don't know what I would have done this weekend if you weren't helping." Wendy set the edge of a can against an electric can opener. "Saturday evenings are hectic enough when everyone is here."

Abby thought she was exaggerating her importance. Even shorthanded, Wendy ran the kitchen efficiently. While they worked, they reminisced. Abby reminded her of the time she'd siphoned gas out of Guy's truck so they'd be stuck alone for a while.

Unabashedly, Wendy admitted, "I'd do anything to get his attention."

"It worked."

"Amazing, isn't it?" Wendy said on a laugh.

They worked for nearly another hour, but they had fun talking about old times. After finishing the pies, Abby peeked into the dining room. Austin was gone, but Sam and Laura hadn't left.

His head bent close to Laura's, Sam laughed at something her aunt had said, and his huge hand enveloped hers. They seemed so engrossed in each other. Abby realized how long it had been since she'd been that absorbed in what a man was saying to her. "Aunt Laura," she said as she approached the table, "do you know where Austin went?"

Laura looked up at her. "He was quite excited about seeing the rooster," she said.

"Last I saw him," Sam cut in, "he was going out the door with Jack."

Again? Abby managed not to frown until she was walking away. At some moment, when Jack was with Austin, would he sense the boy was his son?

After questioning a ranch hand about Jack's whereabouts, Abby learned he'd been seen in the barn. Inside, she wandered along the horse stalls, stilling as she heard first Austin's then Jack's voice.

"Do you want it to go in here?" her son was asking.

"That's right," Jack answered. "Move the hay from here to the bin."

Abby watched Austin working beside his father. Pitchfork in hand, he poked it into a mound of hay. She thought she'd been quiet. But in a sudden move, Austin swung around and faced her with the pitchfork prongs.

"Be careful with that," Jack told him.

"I will." Beaming, he resumed the task Jack had given him. "We're working real hard," he told Abby.

"I can see that."

Jack hadn't been surprised by the boy's willingness to work. He was Abby's son. She had never been pure fluff. During one afternoon, he'd been sunk as he watched her back up a team and keep it steady while hay was stacked. It was hard work even for a man, but that was Abby. She would try her hand at everything from making biscuits to herding the cattle.

Abby waited until Austin moved into a distant stall, then spoke low to Jack so only he heard. "We need to talk."

Definitely she had something on her mind, Jack guessed by her give-me-your-attention-now tone. He set down the grain and leaned a hand against a post.

Abby saw a softness in his eyes she remembered well. How could she have believed that it would be simple to feel unaffected around him? "Jack, why did you tell Austin that you'd take him fishing?"

He stared at her mouth, remembered her taste even now. "You don't want him to go?"

"No. He's excited about going," she said a little grudgingly as she realized how ungrateful she'd nearly sounded.

Despite the softening of her voice, he saw the challenge in her eyes. Though a delicate-looking woman, she was strong, her own person.

Abby made herself meet his stare, felt the pull, strong and insistent. "I want to know why you asked him."

Looking down, he yanked a handkerchief from his back pocket and wiped his hands. "Why shouldn't I?"

"Jack—"

"Abby—" He mocked her exasperated tone. "The answer to your question is simple. Out here there's an unspoken understanding. When someone does a favor for you, you do something for them. You've been helping us in the kitchen, so I wanted to do something for your boy.'' Sam would have smiled at hearing Jack say ''helping us.''

''So that's why?''

''We're taking your time away from him. It didn't seem right that he should get the short end of the stick because you'd offered to help out.'' Both puzzled and amused, he studied her thoughtfully. ''He's a good boy, Abby. He's polite, respectful, appreciative. You raised a son you can be proud of.''

''Thank you.'' He'd been easy to raise. She and Austin had always understood each other. Because of perfect compatibility, they rarely butted heads or had words of disagreement. She knew she was lucky. The funny thing about their harmonious relationship was how much Austin's temperament and disposition were like Jack's. He was his father's son. And as she'd gotten along with Jack, she'd enjoyed a similar rapport with his son.

''I did what you said,'' Austin announced with his return. Eagerness brightened his face. ''Can we go now?''

Jack was looking forward to the afternoon of fishing as much as the boy was. On the road for months, he hadn't fished since last summer. ''We're ready.''

''Are you coming with us, Mom?''

Clearly her son wanted her to accompany them. He was still young enough to like his mother's company, even seek it out. "Yes, if I'm invited. I don't need to go back to the kitchen until this evening."

Jack grinned at her words. "You're invited."

Austin scanned his surroundings for a place to set the pitchfork. "I always have to do my chores first, before I can play."

"What kind of chores?" Jack asked. He took the pitchfork from him and touched his shoulder to urge him toward the door.

Abby didn't miss the ease of the moment between them.

"Mom has me take out the garbage," Austin replied. "I don't like the job." He led the way outside. "It smells, but she said if I have a dog someday, I'll have to clean up after him, and that smells, too."

Jack chuckled. More than once, the kid had made him laugh. "Yeah, she's right. You want a dog?"

"I can't have one now." Walking between them, he glanced up at Abby. "'Cause we live in an apartment."

Abby estimated it would take another five years to afford the down payment for a house. While her mind had drifted with the private thought, a ranch hand had fallen into step with Jack.

"Some fellow selling feed says Sam ordered it," the man said. "Sam went to town, and we don't have a note from him about it. What should we do?"

Jack doubted Sam had placed the order. He'd bought feed only from Len Jensen's Feed and Grain in town for the past twenty-five years. Scowling, he saw Guy coming close. "Tell him no."

Guy waited until the ranch hand was out of hearing range. "Like it or not, you can't get away from it. To the employees, you'll always be the boss, too. Did Sam talk to you yet about staying?"

Jack stared out at the open rangeland. How, with all this space around him, could he feel so crowded?

Abby tried not to look interested in what they were discussing. She even pretended to direct Austin's attention toward the hawk circling nearby.

"He won't," Jack answered.

"He'll have to."

Jack wasn't in the mood for this conversation, but he planned to end it once and for all. "Why will he have to?"

"Because Uncle Ray wants to retire."

With a shrug, Jack brushed aside his comment. "Sam's got a problem then, doesn't he?"

Guy didn't respond, and even after he walked away, Abby kept quiet. It was clear that Jack was still clinging to the freedom to travel on a whim with no responsibilities burdening him. But unlike a drifter who had no purpose, no destination in his wanderings, Jack always knew where he was headed—to wherever the next rodeo was.

Jack mentally swore. He had no intention of being ambushed into changing his plans. He was here for the wedding. Two weeks. No more. Then he was rejoining the rodeo circuit. "You know what?" he said to the boy beside him. "Before we leave, we need to get something."

"What do we need?" Austin raised his face to

Jack. For a split second, he looked so much like Abby that something tightened in Jack's chest.

"Food. We need to get some food. Can't go fishing without cookies and—"

"Candy," Austin finished for him.

"And fruit," Abby cut in, now that her son's best interest was at stake, not to mention her pocketbook, as she thought about dentist bills.

"Candy bars used to be your life's blood," Jack said in a low voice when Austin had moved to a corral post to retrieve the cowboy hat that he'd gotten earlier from Sam.

"A conscience comes with motherhood. I even know the pyramid order."

Humor laced his voice. "Pyramid order?"

"Of foods." Abby sent him a withering look for not taking her seriously. "You know, so much fat, protein, carbohydrates, and…" She paused because he lost it and chuckled. "Never mind."

His smile lingered. He never doubted she'd be a super mother someday. He remembered how she'd cared for a motherless calf they'd had that summer she'd worked at the ranch. She'd practically lived in the barn to baby it.

"I suppose it's useless to talk about the nutritional value of food to someone who consumes enough biscuits and sausage gravy to feed five men," she said.

He fought another grin. "You still are prone to exaggerating."

Abby didn't miss the teasing look in his eyes.

"Isn't Boston supposed to have great baked beans?" he said.

"There are other things of more importance than food."

He played along, enjoying the nothing conversation. "Like what?"

"Beacon Hill. Boston Public Gardens. The Boston Common."

"The Boston Red Sox?"

Abby felt a laugh tickling her throat. "So, in your many travels, when you think of Albuquerque—"

"Indian fry bread."

"And Milwaukee?"

A desire simply to touch her, her hand, a strand of her hair, her cheek, stormed him. "Beer."

"You're impossible." With a finger, Abby beckoned Austin to join them.

"Do you like ham-and-cheese sandwiches?" Jack asked when Austin scurried to his side.

"With mayonnaise," Austin told him. "I had a friend whose mom made them with catsup." He stuck out his tongue to indicate his distaste.

Jack presented the proper scowl. "They really tasted bad?"

"Gross."

Abby couldn't help smiling. The chattering went on after they reached the kitchen.

"Do you like milk?" Austin questioned.

Abby sent Jack a you-had-better look.

Standing before the opened refrigerator, Jack handed a package of ham to Austin. "Oh, sure."

Austin wrinkled his nose. "I don't. But Mom sometimes lets me make chocolate milk. That's really good," he said, following Jack to one of the counters, a loaf of bread dangling from his hand.

At the sink, Abby washed grapes. Beside her, Wendy kept sneaking glances at them while she tossed a huge bowl of salad for dinner.

"Do you like chocolate-chip or oatmeal cookies?" Austin asked.

Jack lathered mayonnaise on bread while Austin placed layers of cheese and ham between the slices of bread. "Chocolate-chip and sandwich cookies, too." He bent his head and spoke quietly, conspiratorially, to Austin as if about to reveal world-shattering information. "I like to open them and eat the frosting first."

"Me, too," Austin whispered back.

"Fruit is packed," Abby called to them.

"Bag them," Jack said about the made sandwiches.

Austin sealed the plastic sandwich bags. "No cookies?"

"Got that covered," Jack assured him, and produced a plastic bag filled with chocolate-chip cookies.

Abby finished packing cans of soda, along with the sandwiches, grapes and cookies, into a picnic basket. Something swelled within her. She wouldn't—couldn't—allow too many days like this. It was as if the three of them were a family.

* * *

Jack drove along a back road, past the ranch complex and a meadow of wildflowers, to a small lake surrounded by clusters of trees. The sun had lowered a bit, casting shadows on the land. The glow spread across the distant jagged cliffs, changing the sandy red and green colors to silver and blue.

In the north, fluffy gray clouds gathered. Standing outside the truck, Abby scanned the darkening sky. "It looks as if it will rain again."

Dropping the tailgate, Jack eyed the sky. "Everyone wants more. They've had a drought."

He'd been home less than a few days, but with that one comment, he revealed that he'd caught up to months of life at the ranch.

With Austin alongside him, he lifted the fishing poles out of the back of the truck and handed one to him. "Did you know your mom is good at this?"

A look that carried a mixture of surprise and incredulity slid over the boy's face. "Is she really?"

"She won a fishing contest."

Austin's eyes went wider. "You won a fishing contest, Mom?"

She mentally groaned. It had been a local contest with only a dozen contestants.

Before she could downplay the achievement, Jack continued. "She won a trophy, too."

"A trophy? Wow!"

"She always got the biggest fish." Squatting, Jack bent his head and stared into his tackle box.

"Not always," Abby insisted. She moved behind him, and over his shoulder she searched in the box for a lure, a favorite purple and yellow salamander. "I always—"

"Liked this one," Jack finished for her, handing the squiggly rubber lure to her. "I remember."

"This is the first time I've been fishing since I left here." They'd gone fishing two days before he'd shattered her heart. Oh, what was the point in revisiting the past? She nudged the memory aside, not wanting to spoil the day.

Jack settled with Abby under a giant oak while Austin walked along the bank. He thought the boy seemed content and happy, but how much had his mother sacrificed to make that life for him? "How did you finish your education, Abby?"

Abby swung a look at him, nearly running the hook through her finger. Reliving that time meant sharing with him the months before she'd had Austin. She stared down at her fingertip. "What do you mean?"

"You left here, had the boy?" Not too much time had passed before she'd gotten pregnant. So much for love eternal, Jack reflected. It obviously hadn't taken her long to forget him. But why wouldn't she have? He'd never promised anything. He'd never given her reason to hope he would change his mind about what he wanted out of life.

"I had him after I graduated." She didn't bother to add that his birth hadn't been months afterward. Abby thanked fate. Timing had been in her favor. She'd taken finals the week before her baby was due. On the last day of school, six days before her due date, as she'd walked out of her medieval history class, she'd felt the first contraction. She'd gone to the hospital, had Austin. Four days later, she graduated. If Jack asked what Austin's birth date was, he would know the truth. Austin was closer to eight than six. Proof existed if Jack wanted it.

With Austin's approach, Jack finished hooking the little boy's line. "Your mom picked a good lure for you. I always catch fish when I use it."

Settling beside him, Austin frowned at the wiggly plastic neon-colored worm on his hook. "Do you want it?"

The boy had his mother's tender heart, Jack mused with a glance Abby's way. She was staring down at her son with a pleased smile. "Thanks, Austin. But you use it this time. I can use it anytime."

Like any mother who hoped her child wasn't disappointed, Abby did some wishful thinking that Austin would catch a fish today. "Did you promise Wendy that we'd bring back some trout?"

Jack cast his line. "She expects chili, not fish. I'm supposed to make a big pot of chili for tomorrow's ranchers' meeting."

Chili was his specialty. He'd won several contests with his recipe.

"Men don't cook," Austin piped in.

Jack made brief eye contact with Abby, saw her glower. "Who told you that?" he asked.

"Traci's dad."

"Traci's a friend from school," Abby explained.

She liked the girl, but thought her father needed a few lessons in modern thinking.

"Traci's dad is wrong," Jack said. He might have said more, but Austin's pole arched. "You got something on your line!"

"Mom! Mom!" His face flushed with excitement, Austin scrambled to a stand. "I got something. Mom, I caught a fish."

Jack didn't offer to help. "Reel it in," he told him.

Thrilled for her son, Abby was standing now with Austin. "Bring it in, honey."

She looked cute, laughing, standing beside her son and offering encouragement.

The boy's face glowed as he brought the fish to the water's surface. Wiggling, it slapped at the water, fighting for its freedom. He reeled it up, but as the fish kept twisting on the line, he frowned. "Can I let it go?"

Abby knew her son's sensitivity about animals. If a child's preferences determined his life's work, Austin would end up as a veterinarian. "Since we're not going to eat it, we should let it go," she suggested.

Jack grinned over Austin's head at Abby, then looked back at the boy. "Do you want me to?" As if eager to do just that, Austin nodded. While Jack took hold of the fish, then gently eased the hook out of its mouth, Austin never left his side.

"Is it okay?"

"It's okay. Watch," Jack said, and let the fish go. Back in the water, it swam quickly out of sight.

Now that he knew it hadn't been harmed, delight sparkled in Austin's eyes again. "That was fun." As he'd do with a new friend, he reached for Jack's hand to get his attention. "Want a sandwich, Jack?"

"You bet." He'd never had contact with any child except Jodi, and she was still so little that a dry diaper and a fresh bottle were all she wanted. The boy demanded more, but he also gave more, making Jack laugh, warming him with an unexpected comment.

As Austin raced toward the truck, Abby set down her fishing pole. "I'd better help him, or the sandwiches will be food for the ants."

They'd been intimate, lovers. She should have been relaxed with him, but Jack sensed she was nervous again. "Are you going to run every time we're alone?"

Her chin shot up. "I'm not running."

"Tell me." He brushed a knuckle across her cheek. After the kiss last night, every moment he'd known with her was a part of him again. "Tell me what you feel. Really feel."

Abby drew in a calming breath. If he wanted honesty, so be it. "I won't deny that a part of me has always felt that we left something unfinished because of how you went away."

Beneath the softness in her voice, he heard her anger.

"But you humiliated me." There, she'd said it.

He couldn't waltz in and out of her life on a whim. "Everyone knew you'd left me without a look back. I'd been wearing my heart on my sleeve. Do you really think I would want to do that again?"

That night he'd been numb, so caught up in his own pain that his only thought had been distancing himself from his father.

Abby raised a hand as a breeze, warm and calm, tossed her hair and visually searched for Austin. Outside the truck he was struggling to open a can of soda. "I'd been looking for you when I ran into Ray," she said to Jack. "He told me you left. Just left. I couldn't believe you'd do that to me." No excuse he would give her would matter. The hurt, the heartache, still existed within her.

He caught her arm as she started to move away. "Do you think leaving you, hurting you, was something I planned?"

"I don't know. I only knew I couldn't stay, couldn't face everyone. At daybreak, I went to Sam." He'd looked so sad, Abby recalled. "I told him that I couldn't keep working for him."

"What did he tell you?"

"He said you'd left because of a fight with him. It had nothing to do with me."

For that he owed his father a thank-you. "But you didn't believe him?"

She released a mirthless laugh. "I was young, I was hurting." She'd given her heart to someone who hadn't cared.

"I never meant to hurt you, Abby."

It didn't matter if that was the truth. That he'd left without her, without even a goodbye, had devastated her. She pulled free of his hand as Austin came close with cans in his hands.

"Want a soda, Mom?"

"Thank you, honey." She took the can, then strolled to the truck for the picnic basket.

Everything had been so mixed up years ago, Jack reflected. From the beginning, they'd both known Abby wouldn't stay. And back then, guilt about his mother dying when he was born was a part of him. He wouldn't have wanted Abby to stay, get serious about him.

"Mom likes cucumber sandwiches," Austin said, grabbing his attention.

Jack dropped to the ground near the blanket they'd spread earlier. "She likes jelly and cheese on toast, too."

Abby heard his comment and frowned as she saw a quizzical look come into her son's eyes.

"How'd you know that?" Austin asked, plopping down beside Jack.

Joining them, Abby knelt and unpacked the picnic basket. She wasn't thrilled that they were talking about her as if she wasn't there.

"Your mom and I were good friends."

Austin sent a puzzled look up at Abby. "Aren't you still?"

Abby unwrapped a sandwich and handed it to him. She knew his tendency to interrogate if something bothered him. "Of course we are." To give him any other answer meant dozens of questions.

Seeming satisfied with that answer, Austin dug into the picnic basket for the bag of potato chips she'd packed.

With his back against a tree trunk, Jack stretched out his legs and popped the tab on a can of soda. "Have you seen the movie about the monkey that plays basketball?" he asked Austin.

Abby's head snapped up. When had he become aware of kids' movies?

Eyes brightening in anticipation, Austin shook his head. "It's supposed to be real good."

Sensing where the conversation was going, Abby took control of the moment with a reminder. "I can't be going off to the movies. I promised to help in the kitchen. Remember?"

Jack aimed a question at Austin. "Would you want to go with me?"

"Could I, Mom?"

Abby started to protest. "I couldn't ask you to—"

Jack ended his fascination with her lips. "I'm asking Austin."

Austin's cheeks reddened with pleasure. "Please, Mom. Pul-eeze."

Jack, what are you doing? With Austin's pleading eyes on her, she nodded. "Yes, okay." Even though she planned not to get involved with Jack, it wasn't fair to take away Austin's fun.

''Whoopee. Thanks, Mom.'' Exuberantly, Austin hugged her, nearly knocking her over.

Abby managed a smile. Too many soft feelings for Jack were a breath away. If she'd learned anything today, it was that trouble was ahead if they spent any more cozy afternoons like this.

Jack spent an enjoyable evening with the boy. The movie had provided plenty of laughs, and he and Austin stuffed themselves on buttered popcorn and candy.

Back at the ranch by nine o'clock, Jack waited on the back porch steps at the lodge while Austin checked in with Abby. For now, he'd decided to give her the space she wanted, but he planned to have his say. Hurting her had been the last thing he'd meant to do.

''Mom's still helping Wendy,'' Austin announced in unison with the slam of the screen door, then took a seat on the top step beside Jack.

Old habits were hard to break. When he was a kid, the back porch steps had been Jack's favorite thinking spot.

Sitting close, Austin rattled on with childish delight about the movie they'd seen, then about the ''humongous'' jar of pickles that he'd eyed in the kitchen minutes ago. ''I ate only three of them. Mom said I'd get a bellyache if I had more.''

''Moms are pretty smart that way.''

''My mom is pretty, isn't she?''

Jack restrained a smile. Was the kid matchmaking, handpicking a guy for his mom? Jack couldn't help feeling flattered that Austin was considering him. "I think so."

"Do you like girls?"

"Most of them."

"I don't. Except Traci."

Once again Jack held back a smile. Abby had told him that Traci's claim to fame was being able to play shortstop. "You will," he assured the boy.

"Uh-uh."

"You like your mom, don't you?"

"Yes," Austin replied.

"Well, she's one."

"I'm what?" Abby questioned as she walked toward them. She'd overheard the last few comments, but more than their words, it was what she saw that weakened her. Austin had his shoulder snug against Jack's arm. Her son's face was full of joy.

Jack winked at Austin before lifting his gaze to Abby. "You're pretty."

Austin stood and started down the steps to her. "We both think so."

Abby accepted the compliment graciously. "Thank you."

"Can I watch TV tonight?" Austin asked.

"It's time for bed," she replied with a shake of her head.

"Aw, Mom."

Abby ruffled his hair. "Say goodnight, Austin."

Laughing, he dodged her hand. "Thanks again, Jack, for taking me to the movie."

"Anytime."

Abby saw the look in Jack's eyes and knew he meant what he said.

As if he'd forgotten something, Austin dashed back up the stairs. "Bye, Jack."

A weak, queasy sensation settled in the pit of her stomach as she watched her son high-five Jack. Her heart felt heavy suddenly. It was so obvious Jack would be a good father. Abby shut her eyes to banish the thought. There was no point in even thinking of him in those terms. She'd burned that bridge long ago.

Chapter Five

Her mind troubled, Abby was glad to get away from the ranch for a little while the next morning. Reading one of his comic books, Austin had been quiet through most of the drive to town. Though she had a dress fitting, she'd promised him an ice-cream soda afterward. Earlier, she'd written a few promised postcards to co-workers at the newspaper, then wrapped a present, a peach peignoir, for the lingerie shower planned for her aunt tomorrow.

Her thoughts turned to Jack and her son. A lack of male companionship was a logical excuse for Austin enjoying himself with Jack, but Abby rarely stuck her head in the sand and ignored the truth. Her son hadn't responded the same way to any other man she'd dated. With no knowledge that they were father and son, Jack and Austin had become friends quickly.

Squinting against the Saturday-morning sun, she braked for a red light at the edge of town. She should have told Jack when she'd first realized she was pregnant. She'd planned to that night eight summers ago. Then she learned he'd left. The idea of chasing him down had emphasized that Austin's whole life would be spent trailing after his father. How could he visit him in hotels, this city tonight, another city tomorrow?

So despite the ranch and decades of McShanes rooted to the Double M, Jack, by choice, had no home to offer his son. And Austin was what mattered most. His feelings, his happiness, his security.

Austin's voice interrupted her thoughts. "It's real neat, Mom."

"Yes, it is." Storekeepers had maintained the look of a frontier town to please the tourists. Hitching posts lined the street in front of the shops. Cruising along the main street, she searched for the town's only bridal shop.

Beside her, Austin shifted on the seat and peered out the window. "Where's the ice-cream parlor?"

"Over there." Abby pointed. She could see it hadn't changed. Though obviously painted since she'd last been there, it still had a Gay Nineties decor. Next to it stood an old-fashioned general store with an old-style cash register.

At the north edge of town, gas stations dotted every corner and a shopping mall stretched for nearly a city block. Wedged between a florist and a shoe repair shop was the bridal salon. The owner, according to Wendy, was a loquacious, sweet woman and self-appointed town matchmaker. Abby found that to be true. For during her fitting, the shop owner mentioned the names of several eligible bachelors in town, including Jack.

Abby distracted the woman by raving about the dress her aunt had chosen for her to wear. High at the throat, lacey and tea-length, the soft blue dress was lovely, feminine—romantic.

"You looked so nice in that dress. Pretty enough to be the bride," the woman told Abby after she'd changed and emerged from a back room.

"Thank you," Abby responded.

Hearing them, Austin closed his comic book and sprung from his chair. "Are we going for ice cream now?"

"Right now," she said, meeting him at the door. Though they could have walked to the ice-cream parlor, Abby drove. She found a parking space only two stores away from it. Head bent, she ambled beside Austin and dropped her sunglasses into her shoulder bag.

"Mom, look, there's Guy."

Abby looked up to see him outside the hardware store.

"Hey, Abby. Whatcha doing in town?" he asked, moving toward them.

"I came for a fitting on my dress for the wedding…'' Her voice trailed off as she noticed who had accompanied Guy to town.

"Jack!" Austin yelled, and dashed over to him.

From his position near Guy's truck, Jack sent her a long, slow smile. One that made her nervous.

"Can't believe Sam's taking the plunge," Guy was saying. "As long as I've known him, he's been single."

Abby nodded absently, more interested in the secretive smile shared by Jack and her son.

Near Jack now, not too gently, Guy elbowed him. "Remember when we were kids, and the widow Sommers decided to pursue him?" Guy swung a grin at Abby. "She believed the way to a man's heart was through his stomach."

"I remember," Jack said, he and Austin moving to join Abby on the sidewalk. "Every day she brought Sam some specialty from her kitchen. I always told her how much my dad loved her food."

Amusement sprang into Guy's voice. "That's funny. Sam was trying to figure out how to stop her, and you were encouraging her."

"She made great pies," Jack replied, as if that was a sufficient reason.

Abby noticed that all during the exchange, Jack repeatedly made eye contact with Austin. What were they up to? she wondered.

Not too discreetly, Guy cast a speculative look at Jack and then at Abby. "I'd better get back to the ranch."

Though Guy moved, Jack didn't budge. Because

her son didn't have a poker face, it occurred to Abby this was not a chance meeting. "Don't you have to leave with—" The hand she'd waved in the direction of Guy's truck fell to her side as Guy backed out of the parking space.

"We didn't come to town together," Jack told her.

Clearly he wasn't moving an inch until she asked him to join them.

Her son, the actor, took center stage and turned appealing eyes up at her. "Jack could come for ice cream, too," he said oh so innocently. "Couldn't he, Mom?"

Abby didn't bother to protest.

The ice-cream parlor looked as it had almost a decade ago. Clean. White. The only splash of color came from the wrought-iron chairs with their peppermint-striped cushioned seats.

Upon entering, Jack waved to an older couple seated at another table with their granddaughter. "Remember the Williamsons?"

Abby settled on the chair he'd pulled out for her. "Yes," she said, recalling that Mr. Williamson once ran the ice-cream store. "Did he ever let his son take over?"

"Three years ago." As Austin took a seat, Jack lifted the boy's cowboy hat from his head. "Want the usual?" he asked her.

"What's the usual, Mom?" Austin's eyes were

fixed on a banana split someone at the next table was eating.

"A chocolate soda."

"With lots of whipped cream?" Jack rounded a look at a waiter in a white jacket and straw hat who was suddenly standing beside him.

"Lots," Abby assured him.

"I want that, too, then," Austin said.

Watching the waiter set down water glasses, Abby realized that the last chocolate soda she'd had was here, with Jack.

"Double chocolate?" the waiter asked after Jack ordered three sodas.

Abby couldn't resist. "Double chocolate." She laughed as the waiter walked away. "I'll take a long walk later."

Jack set his and Austin's hats on the chair beside him. "I don't think a few pounds will hurt. You look terrific. In fact, you don't look any different than you did eight years ago."

Abby snuck a look at Austin to see how much of their conversation he was taking in. His nose was buried in a comic book. At seven he apparently thought his favorite superhero's adventures were more interesting than anything happening to his mother.

"Sam said you're having a bridal shower for Laura."

Abby nodded. "We're surprising her with it while you and Sam are at the ranchers' meeting." A hint of a frown veed his eyebrows and she wondered if he was feeling cornered by ranch responsibilities. While that wasn't her concern, her aunt was. "You haven't said more about the wedding."

"There's not much to say." Jack shifted on the chair. "They seem happy, don't they? That's all that really matters."

Abby heard no disapproval in his voice. "So you don't dislike her?"

"I never did, Abby. Who wouldn't like her?" he asked honestly. During the past days, he'd seen Laura's efforts to fit in, helping wherever she was needed, charming guests.

"Someone's waving at you, Jack," Austin informed him.

"Jack!" a woman practically squealed. Tall, bosomy and dressed in short shorts and a T-shirt that bared her midriff, a twenty-something blonde gushed when she reached their table. "You are Jack McShane, aren't you?" With his nod, she swiveled a know-it-all-look at her companion, who was now beside her. "Told you."

An equally tall and well-endowed brunette set a pen and napkin before him. "Could I have your autograph?"

Wide-eyed, Austin stared at both women, especially the one woman's navel ring.

Abby noted that they'd inched closer as if needing to be in Jack's breathing space.

The blonde released a huge sigh that heaved her ample bosom. "We saw you at the rodeo in Prescott."

Abby regarded the woman's adolescent dreamy-eyed look. She supposed rodeo groupies came with the championship buckle he'd won.

Jack scrawled his signature and, delivering a well-practiced smile, he handed the pen and autographed napkin back to the woman.

"I heard you'll be teaching the wilderness-survival class like you used to. I'd just love to join it," the blonde said, her words practically a purr.

What the woman would love was to get closer to Jack, Abby guessed. She was glad to see Austin was again caught up in his hero's battle to save the planet Zentur.

"You got the wrong information," Jack said, wondering who she had gotten it from. Were people in town assuming that since he was back for more than a few days, he was staying permanently? "I won't be teaching the class."

"Oh." The blonde's features drooped with disappointment. "I hope you'll change your mind. If you do—" She set a slip of paper on the table beside Jack's hand and sent him a slow-forming smile. "Call me."

Abby realized that she could have been invisible. What if she'd been Jack's fiancée, or his wife? "Does that happen often?" she asked Jack once the two young women had moved away.

Jack didn't miss the hint of annoyance in her voice. "Often."

"Unbelievable. And you love it."

"I'll take the Fifth on that one."

''Holy cow!'' Austin straightened on his chair as the waiter placed chocolate sodas topped with whipped cream and cherries before them. ''I've never seen a soda this big. You were right, Jack. They make the bigge—'' As if he knew he'd said too much, he slapped a hand over his mouth, his eyes darting to Abby.

Just as she'd thought. This was a planned meeting. With a look from her, Austin sunk his neck lower in his shoulders.

''When did you two talk about the sodas?'' she asked them both.

Jack's eyes danced with devilment. ''We're done for. We've been caught,'' he said to Austin.

''At breakfast, Mom,'' Austin confessed. ''I told Jack we were coming here.''

Jack wasn't going to back off, she realized suddenly. It hadn't mattered what she'd said to him yesterday.

''Did you say your baseball team was called the Blue Jays?'' Jack asked Austin, trying to change the subject.

Mouth full, Austin wagged his head while he swallowed. ''The Orioles.'' He paused in bringing the spoon to his mouth. ''Next spring, I get to play in the minors.''

It was clear to Abby that they'd discussed Little League before this. ''Austin played in T-ball this year,'' she explained, not certain how much Jack had been told.

"I was a shortstop," Austin piped in between slurps on the straw.

Abby had never considered Jack the fatherly type. She didn't think he had the patience needed for dealing with a child. But he'd been sensitive, caring and inordinately patient with Austin whenever he showed him how to do something. It seemed sad to her that he believed he never wanted a child of his own when he was so good with one.

"Mom." Austin leaned toward her and spoke low. "I got to go to the bathroom."

Abby pointed to a nearby door. "It's right there."

After a quick swipe at his mouth with his napkin, he took off.

"He's a great kid, Abby," Jack told her.

"Thank you." She couldn't meet his eyes. She simply couldn't, with so much guilt weighing her down. Maybe she should just tell him the truth. No, she couldn't. It didn't matter that the truth was fair to Jack or that it would alleviate her of guilt. The truth wouldn't be good for Austin. If he learned to love Jack, he'd be hurt. He could live without a father. What he couldn't live with was a father who'd put him second, who'd be absent from his life more than he'd be with him.

Jack leaned forward. "About yesterday—"

Abby waved a hand in the air. "There's nothing more to say."

There was plenty to explain, Jack thought, but he couldn't do it in a public place with Austin due back any moment.

Avoiding his stare, Abby searched for something less personal to discuss. "When I was helping Wendy, she said something about Guy thinking of quitting rodeo." Slowly she ran a fingertip over the rim of the soda glass. Like Jack, Guy seemed obsessed with the danger, needed the thrill. "I never thought he would want to leave the circuit."

"Wendy wants him home." He looked to the door in response to the jingle of the bell above it. A family of four came in. "Wendy thinks Jodi needs her daddy around."

"That's important," Abby agreed. "But what kind of a father will he be if he's forced to stay home?" Her own father, a drummer, had eventually chosen his music over her and her mother.

A tall man with reddish-brown hair and a booming laugh, he had been her world. When he hugged her, she'd always felt so safe, felt as if no one could hurt her, nothing could go wrong. Ironically, the person who made her feel that way was also the one who'd hurt her the most. "I'm happy for them, if it works out."

Out of loyalty, Jack wanted to come to Guy's defense. "You have doubts?"

Abby dipped her spoon back in the soda. "Not really."

He cooled an urge to defend his friend. The conversation wasn't about Guy any longer, Jack guessed. "You were thinking about your father, weren't you?"

"My mother, actually." She'd been a heartbroken

woman who'd never stopped looking for her husband to come back to her. In retrospect, Abby believed her mother had been clingy, too dependent on him. "He hurt her badly. But she should have known he wouldn't settle down forever. Musicians are always on the go, chasing a dream."

Jack heard her unsaid words. Like rodeo cowboys.

"We traveled constantly because he needed to for his job. He'd play for a couple of weeks at a club. Sometimes it would be longer, but never more than a month or two." She'd been young, ten, but not unaware. "One day we checked into a motel in San Jose, California. He left to play at some club, promised to kiss me good-night when he came home, and didn't come back." She looked toward the rest room door. "Guy isn't like my father was," she said in fairness to him. "From what Wendy has told me, he's tried really hard to be with her and Jodi in between rodeos."

Having had his fill of the ice cream and chocolate syrup, Jack set down his spoon. "Do you want me to check on Austin?" he asked as her gaze focused on the bathroom door again.

Abby knew her son well. "Give him a few more minutes. No doubt he got sidetracked. He plays Michael Jordan and shoots balled-up paper towels into the waste basket."

"He's doing that now?"

"Probably," Abby said lightly. She gave Austin the mental count of ten.

On five, he came out of the rest room. Only tables away, he stopped by Chris, the boy he'd met the other day at the ranch. As he made eye contact with Abby, she gave him a silent look of approval that he could stay and talk to the boy.

"Tell me something," Jack began curiously. "After your parents divorced…"

"They were never legally divorced. My mother never stopped believing he'd come back. But I never saw him again. He never called. He acted as if he'd never had a child."

Jack set a forearm on the table. There were questions he hadn't thought to ask the first time she'd told him. "What did your mother tell you?"

All he cares about is his music. "She used to cry a lot when I asked about him, so I stopped. I didn't want to make her sad." On her twelfth birthday, Abby remembered waiting for a birthday card from him. When none came, she convinced herself that he would call. When he didn't, she decided that she no longer had a father, and gave up waiting to hear from him. In her mind, he'd died. "He shouldn't have married. He probably loved us in his own way. Just not enough."

Jack stared at her bare ring finger. Like her own mother, she was raising her child alone. She didn't have a lot of luck with men, Jack reflected. First her father, then him, and finally Austin's father had all left her. "Has it been tough playing supermom?"

Abby inclined her head questioningly. "Supermom?"

"Having a career and raising a child can't be easy."

"I had help." Abby finished the last of her ice cream. "After Austin was born, I went to work at a local paper in Houston. Aunt Laura watched him at her boutique. Then this job in Boston three years ago."

Admiration doubled for her. He'd always known her determination, her tenacity, when she wanted something. Around the ranch, people said that a person with those traits had pioneer spirit. "You've done well for yourself."

"We both have. You're famous now. Was being a four-time world champion a goal?"

As she stood, he took his cue, and rising, he set money on the table. How often had he been somewhere, seen a woman with the same rich copper-colored hair and thought of her? "No, being a five-time winner is," he finally answered.

He'd offered the lighthearted answer, but he knew there might be serious consequences to that decision. While riding Roper that morning, he'd felt the nagging pain in his recently injured knee. "I advise you to consider retirement," the doctor had said the last time he had seen him. But he, not a doctor or anyone else, would decide when he quit rodeo.

"Why do you want to?" she asked.

He could feed her bull about wanting to make history, but the facts were simple. If he quit, he'd have nothing to do. He couldn't come back to the ranch, couldn't resume his job there. He couldn't stand side by side with Sam as if nothing had changed. Eight years ago, any chance of that had been shattered. Lies. He'd never get past how many of them Sam was guilty of. Or how much those lies had changed his life. Always he'd wonder what might have been between him and Abby if things had been different.

"Mom, shouldn't we go?" Austin's voice came from behind her.

"Yes, we should." A check of the time revealed they'd barely make it back to the ranch in time for the craft class.

"What's his hurry?" Jack asked.

"Pottery class," Abby said, watching as Austin ran out to the car and stood by the passenger-side door.

She considered how easy it had been to be with Jack. There should have been tension like yesterday, something, anything, so she wouldn't have felt so comfortable with him.

But it had felt right to be with him again. This was the man who'd given her the most precious gift of her life. This was the man to whom she'd offered not only her body but also her heart. What if she could have this time, even only a couple of weeks with him, what if she could block out everything else?

At the car door, he stood so near that his mouth was only inches from hers. She felt the heat of his breath on her cheek and found herself staring into his eyes, into the dark blueness she thought she would lose herself in.

"Mom, aren't you going to unlock the door?"

Abby mentally shook herself. Before she did something silly, she slipped the key into the lock, then quickly slid behind the steering wheel.

Jack waited for her to roll down the window. Resting a forearm on its edge, he spoke softly. "Don't be afraid to admit what you want, Abby."

She made herself meet his stare. Hadn't she done enough? With one kiss, she'd already revealed everything she'd tried to deny to herself. She still wanted him in a way she'd never wanted any other man. "What if it isn't what I should want?"

"What if it is?" Jack stared at her slightly parted lips until Austin's movement caught his eye. "See you, Austin."

"Thanks for the ice cream. It was really good."

He didn't understand, Abby realized as she watched Jack walk away. Her life was about her son, about caring for her child, it could no longer be about a fantasy that she'd abandoned years ago.

Chapter Six

Abby managed to get Austin back in time for the craft class. He told her that after the class he was going to learn to lasso a bull. Abby doubted that a bull was involved. More likely a calf would dodge the children's ineffectual efforts at tossing the looped end of a rope. After leaving him, she wandered into the kitchen. Over a cup of coffee with Wendy, she finalized arrangements for her aunt's shower.

With time to herself before Wendy needed her help with the barbecue, Abby strolled to the corral where Guy was finishing a rope trick for some guests.

"I'd like to go for a ride," she said to the ranch hand in charge of the guests' horseback riding.

Instead of him, a few minutes later, Guy came from the stable with reins in his hand as he led a horse behind him. "Here you are, Abby. Guessed you might be thinking about a ride."

"Oh, it's Wizard." Abby stared at the bay she'd ridden when she'd been here years ago. Still spry, the beautiful animal with a dark brownish-red coat and a white diamond-shaped mask whinnied with its approach. As if remembering her, the bay's nose poked at Abby's shoulder when she stepped near. She laughed and caught the horse's bridle to bring the silky smooth face close to hers.

Guy gave her the expected advice. "You be careful."

Abby took the reins from him. "I will." Mounting, she eyed the horse trail that led toward the foot of the mountains. She set the horse at a slow pace until they cleared the ranch buildings, then gave the bay full rein.

She'd needed this ride, needed to feel the wind blowing through her hair. In the middle of clusters of straggly bushes and wispy desert shrubs, she saw a coyote. Sheepish at being seen, it scurried in a different direction.

When the ranch buildings disappeared from sight, she rode along a fenced, dirt lane. For nearly an hour, she let the bay dawdle, pick its way through a meadow of bright sunflowers and past a herd of white-faced Herefords. Relaxed, she looked beyond a sandy wash, past craggy canyons. This land was a legacy to Austin. By being silent, and not telling

Jack about Austin, she was stealing it from him, wasn't she?

No matter how much she wanted to forget the past, she couldn't. She'd kept the truth to herself because she'd truly believed that Jack wouldn't want to know he was a father. For most of his life, he'd carried the burden of guilt, believing his birth had caused his mother's death. She remembered how adamant he'd been about no marriage. He wouldn't marry a woman because he would never give her a child, never risk any woman's life.

Back then, Abby had tried to convince him that most women who had children survived. He'd turned a deaf ear to her. A careful man, he'd used protection when they made love. One time, a few weeks before he left, before she left, they'd gone camping.

While crossing a brook, they'd begun splashing each other. Laughing, they'd shed wet clothes. They'd made love quickly, with heat, with love but without protection. And she'd thought about what they'd done almost immediately after. She'd thought about it, and had had no regrets. She'd been in love, knew a child conceived in love would never be considered a mistake. From the second she'd guessed she might be pregnant, she wanted her baby.

But Jack hadn't. So what if he did know now? What would change? He lived a life on the road, traveling from rodeo to rodeo. That wouldn't change just because he learned he had a son. Austin would get nothing more than a part-time father.

Returning to the ranch, she slid from the saddle and planned to walk Wizard into the stables. Before she'd taken a few steps, one of the ranch hands met her and took the bay from her. Abby thanked him and scanned the corral area, expecting to see Austin perched on the corral fence, but she didn't see him anywhere.

"If you're looking for Austin, he went with Jack to repair the fence around the swimming pool," Guy said on his way past her.

"Thanks." Abby did an about-face, then strode toward the swimming pool to find Austin and Jack. With passing smiles at guests, she crossed the lawn at the back of the lodge. As she neared the pool, where several guests were basking in the sun, she saw nothing wrong with the pool fence.

She assumed they'd already repaired it. Playing sleuth, Abby checked her watch, then opened the back screen door to enter the kitchen. At two o'clock, Austin usually agonized about dinner being too far away and clutched his stomach to convince her that he needed cookies or he would waste away to nothing.

Abby guessed right.

Sitting at the kitchen table, he was dunking a vanilla wafer into a glass of milk. Beside him, in a high chair, Wendy and Guy's daughter cooed as she gummed a cookie.

"Hi, Mom," Austin said. A milk mustache bordered his upper lip.

"Hi, yourself. I've been looking for you."

"I've been real busy. First, I had to help one of the little kids get down from the corral fence."

Abby maintained a sober expression as she recalled that the children of several of the guests were probably six months to a year younger than him. "That was nice, Austin."

He sent her a grin. "And then I had to help Jack repair a fence."

"Yes, I heard."

At the sink, washing vegetables, Wendy smiled over her shoulder at them. Nearby, one assistant was breading chicken for a menu appetizer. Another one was cutting tips off fresh string beans. Noticing that her son had four cookies left, Abby settled on a chair adjacent to him. "What else did you do?"

"I was going to go horseback riding, but Jack said I couldn't go without checking with you first."

The idea of Austin horseback riding rushed a shiver of fear through her.

"Jack said he has a horse I could ride."

It was one thing for Jack to suggest fishing, but she would decide when Austin was old enough for horseback riding. "We'll see."

"That usually means no," he mumbled in a disgruntled tone.

Abby caught Wendy's grin before she stepped outside, and nearly plowed into Sam in her haste down the steps. "Have you seen Jack?" she asked the older man.

"He's in the stable." Sam released his steadying grip on her. "Do you know where your aunt is?"

"Sorry, no, I don't." She kept walking, and realized, steps from him, that she might have appeared rude. But she had to talk to Jack.

Entering the stable, she walked down the row of stalls until she found Jack in the last one, scrutinizing the hoof of a gray quarter horse.

"I need to talk to you," she said, raising her eyes from his sun-browned hands holding the horse's hoof steady.

Standing, Jack pulled a rag from his pocket.

Abby met his questioning blue eyes. "Austin told me that you said you had a horse he could ride. He's never ridden a horse, Jack." *He's only seven.*

"I was thinking about Rainbow for him," he replied.

Rainbow. Abby remembered the white, tan and brown horse. She was so sweet. In fact, Rainbow had been the mare she'd first ridden when she'd come to work at the ranch.

"Your boy could ride her. She's aging. Docile, too. Content to go slow." He pointed and turned Abby's attention to the horse behind her. "Aren't you, girl?" Jack patted the mare's rump affectionately. "Can I teach him?"

"Can he, Mom?" Austin asked unexpectedly behind her, obviously having followed.

As Austin sidled close, she placed a hand on her son's slim shoulder and smiled down at him. "Yes."

Ecstatic, he let out a loud cheer and wrapped his arms around her waist. "Boy, Mom." Unbridled glee flushed his cheeks. "Wait until I tell everyone at home that I rode a horse."

Abby pressed a kiss to the top of his head. Even as she held him close, she felt as if she was letting him go.

A half hour later, Abby sat perched on the top rail of the corral fence and watched Jack walking beside Rainbow as Austin rode the horse around the corral. She should have known Jack would teach Austin to ride before he would let him out of the corral. A cliché slipped into her thoughts when Austin rode by and waved. He was definitely sitting tall in the saddle.

Late-afternoon sunshine glaring in her eyes, she glanced at her watch. With a promise to return and help in the kitchen, she had no choice but to leave. "I have to go, honey," she said, and waved.

Cautiously, he raised one of his hands from its grip on the saddle horn to wave back. "Bye, Mom."

"Bye," she called back, pleased for him.

"You three look good together," Wendy said as a greeting when Abby entered the kitchen. Standing by the window, she had a bird's-eye view of the corral.

Abby reached for one of the bib aprons hanging on a hook in the short hallway that led to the pantry, but she, too, could see the corral, see Jack and Austin. Father and son. They looked so content with each other. "What do you want me to do?" she asked instead of responding to Wendy's comment.

As if she'd never said anything about them, Wendy said breezily, "You'll be sorry you asked."

Nearby, several employees shared a smile. Nonstop, they and the kitchen staff of half a dozen worked for the next three hours.

By six that evening, Abby stood with Wendy and other kitchen help behind a long table of food. With a metal plate in hand, guests formed a line and were hustled along to receive huge spoonfuls of beans and potato salad, slices of barbecue beef, an ear of corn and a biscuit.

Jack stole Austin from Laura and Sam to give them time alone, and were among the nearly two hundred people served dinner in fifteen minutes. Seated at one of the picnic tables set up for the barbecue, he found himself smiling as he watched Austin scarff down dinner and then a slice of blueberry pie.

Under the pavilion, a country band played music. Jack knew the program. Guests enjoyed a night of fun and music under the stars. In between the music, they were treated to comedy skits, mostly ones that poked fun at cowboys.

"There's my mom." Austin waved in Abby's direction. "Do you see her?"

"I see her." He hadn't taken his eyes off her. As the evening wound down, he thought about how often he'd been in a crowd like this, and wish he'd seen her face.

"Hey, Jack." Head bent, Austin was fishing for

something in his shirt pocket. ''I got bubble gum.''
He produced a small pink square. ''Want some?''

Jack checked a smile. ''No, thanks.'' Every time
he was with the boy, he felt closer to Abby.

''Know what I'd like?'' Austin said.

That was easy for Jack to answer. The boy longed
for a pet. ''A dog.''

Austin cracked his gum. ''There's something else
I'd like.''

Jack expected something outlandish, like an elephant. ''What do you want?''

''A brother.''

''A br—'' Unprepared, Jack took a moment and
cleared his throat. He'd heard deadly seriousness in
the boy's voice. ''Does your mom know?''

Austin blew a bubble. ''She said I couldn't have
that, either. I know we can't have a dog 'cause we
live in an apartment. But I could have a brother.
There isn't any rule about not allowing babies.''

Jack stifled a grin. So he understood a brother
wouldn't arrive ready to play ball with him. ''You
wouldn't mind a baby?''

''I know they're kind of noisy. I could kind of
pat its back—real gentle,'' he added. ''That's what
I saw Traci's mom do to her baby.''

That would explain where the idea came from,
Jack assumed.

''Sometimes they're stinky.'' Austin made a face.
''But Mom has to change the diaper. I'm too young
to do that.''

Good sense made Jack steer Austin to a safer

topic. "About the dog. If you could have one, what kind would you like?"

"What kind?" He slipped his hand in Jack's as they stood to leave. His eyes danced with his smile. "Any kind."

By ten-thirty, the evening was over. Abby finished helping with cleanup in the kitchen, then she stepped into the lobby. Seeing her aunt standing by the window, she approached her. "It's raining?" Abby said, surprised because she hadn't heard any raindrops while she was in the kitchen.

"It started raining five minutes ago. Sam assures me it wouldn't dare rain on our wedding day."

Abby touched her shoulder. "This is the rainy season. We can have rain every night for weeks. But the wedding is in the afternoon. Storms don't usually come in until late evening," Abby said, ridiculously trying to offer some kind of reassurance about the weather several days away.

"Cross your fingers for me that the weather stays predictable."

"I'll cross fingers and toes," Abby said, drawing her aunt's laugh.

"Tonight was fun, wasn't it?"

"Yes." Even working, Abby had had fun. "Have you seen Austin?"

"He went out back." Laura abandoned her fascination with the stormy sky to look at Abby. "Obviously he takes after his mother."

She'd always enjoyed walking in the rain. "I

didn't have time to tell you earlier, but I love the dress you chose for me.''

Laura's face lit with a smile. ''Oh, I'm so glad. So you got the final fitting on your dress?''

''Yes, earlier.'' Abby stepped away and followed a path to the door. It would be like Austin to be sitting on a playground swing and letting the rain pour on him. She recalled the walks she'd taken with Jack in the rain. With parents who thought getting wet was a fun thing to do, how could Austin not feel the same?

How many other traits had Austin inherited from both of them? She knew he was tenacious, a quality she and Jack carried, and he was curious like her, as well as stubborn like Jack. He could be almost bullheaded when he thought he was right. He also had a marvelous sense of humor. Another attribute of Jack's.

Steps away from the back screen door, she heard voices. Like the other evening, as if they belonged together, Jack and Austin sat side by side beneath the shelter of the back porch. As the door squeaked open they both looked over their shoulders at her.

''Hi, Mom.''

''Hi.'' She eyed the smudge of chocolate on Austin's cheek.

''Are you exhausted?'' Jack asked her. He'd been missing her, wanting to be with her ever since he left her this afternoon.

''Incredibly.'' Abby let the door close behind her. ''I'd forgotten how much work that barbecue was.''

Jack thought she'd made it look easy. She'd taken over as if she'd never stopped helping out.

"I liked it when they sang that funny song about the alligator who wore a saddle," Austin said about the country band of four.

Jack's eyes gleamed with humor. "You said you liked the song about the cactus that talked."

"Both of them."

Squatting beside him, Abby brushed a fingertip against the chocolate on her son's cheek. "I see you had the chocolate cake for dessert."

"I had blueberry pie, too."

"And how did you get two desserts?" she asked leaning back against one of the uprights near him. He sent her a sheepish grin. "Jack gave me his."

They both turned similar looks up at her. If they were looking in a mirror, they would see matching smiles. Abby's heart twisted.

"Mom, can I?" Austin asked emphatically, indicating to Abby that he'd repeated a question.

"Can you do what?"

"Can I watch the movie in the recreation room?"

"What movie?" She'd already decided that it wouldn't hurt him to stay up late one night. She was becoming as bad as her aunt, she reflected. Lately, she found herself indulging him. But she'd been busy helping Wendy and felt a smidgen of guilt leading her.

"The Wolfman Meets Dracula."

Jack restrained a grin. "Scary stuff."

"Yeah," Austin said with utmost seriousness.

"I'll meet you in the lobby when it's over," Abby told him.

"Okay, Mom." Standing, he high-fived Jack before opening the screen door.

Jack expected her to scurry off with some excuse. Instead, concern clouding her eyes, she settled on the step beside him.

"I saw you two together at dinner. He rambles sometimes," she said.

"He talks a lot about dogs." He decided against mentioning their discussion about a brother.

"That's on the top of his wish list."

Jack read distress in her eyes that she couldn't give him the pet. "Ever have a wish list when you were a kid?"

Abby looked away with a frown. Every night she used to wish her father would call. "Nothing my mother could give me." Hugging her knees, she listened to the tapping of the rain against the roof, watched it pelt the ground. As the breeze swept damp air at her, Abby roused herself from an almost dreamy state. "I should go back in. I need to check on Austin—"

"He's watching a movie, Abby."

"I—"

When she stood, so did he.

Before she realized what was happening, he'd slid his hand to her back, and his mouth brushed hers. Her hand fluttered, touched his waist. Her heart pounding, she knew she was close to forgetting what mattered most. She'd loved before and he'd left her.

He hadn't cared about her, not really. But there was no denying what she felt, wanted. On a sigh, she slowly snaked her hand up his back, then drew him closer.

As she felt his hand moving over her, an ache rose within her. It was as if it were years of yesterdays ago. She yearned to be as one with him again, to feel the slick dampness of his flesh beneath her fingertips. She was weak, so weak. He could have her. She knew it, and with the kiss, so did he. But she couldn't go with emotions, couldn't let the kiss warm her, excite her too much.

Before her mouth grew hungrier, she broke the kiss. With effort, not feeling too wise or sensible, she pulled back from him. "I won't lie to you. I might always want you," she murmured, still breathless. "But what I want doesn't matter."

Breathing hard, too, Jack stared at her as she went into the house. Like hell it didn't. For a full moment, he simply stared. Then on a laugh, he went down the stairs, to head home. How in the devil could she say that and walk away?

Chapter Seven

She shouldn't have said that to him, Abby decided. By seven the next evening, she was still fretting about how to act when she saw Jack, and planned to pretend she hadn't said anything.

Fortunately he would be busy at a ranchers' meeting in the living room at Sam's home. While he and Sam were there, Abby sent Austin off to a kids' swimming party, and she joined a room full of neighbors and friends for Laura's lingerie shower. Listening to her aunt's girlish giggle, Abby fought a wave of melancholy. She truly believed if Jack hadn't left, then they would have been married by now.

"Oh, my," Laura said, drawing Abby's attention back to her. Abby's aunt held up another gift, a black teddy. "This is going to supercharge Sam's engine."

"No, I think that red number will," Wendy said about a nightgown that was paper thin.

Laura cast an appreciative look at her opened presents. "All of the lingerie is so beautiful."

Conversation and lighthearted banter went on for another hour. With dinner almost ready, and the ranchers' meeting over, Laura said her thank-yous again, and Abby helped her carry the gifts to her room. When she returned, the shower guests were wandering outside where the others had gathered. Though her help was no longer needed in the kitchen, Abby joined Wendy in the kitchen several minutes later.

Wendy pointed toward the refrigerator. "Would you bring the cake?"

Abby moved around several of the kitchen staff, who were carting out bowls of food, and opened the refrigerator. Inside was an exquisitely decorated, two-layer chocolate cake. "Oh, this looks delicious, Wendy."

Her friend beamed. "I'd hoped to make use of a cake-decorating class I took. This is sort of a dress rehearsal for the wedding cake."

Carefully Abby lifted the cake plate from the shelf. "I bet it will be beautiful."

"I hope so. Anyway, I made this for dessert after the barbecue tonight," she said before leading the way from the kitchen to everyone gathered poolside.

Lanterns and fiery torches illuminated the dining

area. Strumming guitarists entertained guests. The dark water of the pool glimmered beneath the moonlight. The aroma of smoke from the mesquite-wood fire and the spicy tang of barbecue sauce permeated the night.

From several feet away, Orlon Phillips, editor of the local newspaper, yelled a hello and wound his way around some of the guests to reach Abby. "I heard that you work for a big-city newspaper now," he said. "Too bad you're all set there. Your aunt sent Sam that article you wrote for the Houston paper about ranchers' grazing rights. Damn fine article, Abigail. Sure could use someone like you." He tipped his gray head toward hers. "I'll be retiring soon, you know. Need someone to take over my position."

Abby was flattered that he'd even considered her for the editorial job.

Showing the good manners she'd taught him, Austin sidled close and remained silent at her side until Orlon finished talking to her and was whisked away by one of the town's eligible ladies.

Briefly her son talked with excitement about an upcoming rodeo, then pointed to a boy on the other side of the buffet tables. "Mom, I'm going to sit by Chris and eat. Is that okay?"

Abby noticed Chris perched on a log bench. "Go ahead, honey."

"Abby." Wendy was suddenly on the other side of her. "Look over there."

Ever gracious, Abby's Aunt Laura had been

caught in a dance with one of the ranch hands. His arm was pumping hers as he led her in a two-step.

''She'll need to soak her feet tomorrow. He's got a reputation for stepping on them,'' Wendy added with a laugh.

From the edge of the party, Jack made eye contact with Abby. Until that moment, he'd felt alone, he realized. He'd been waiting, watching for her. A hot evening breeze fluttered the soft material of her green print dress as she moved around the pool, nodding hello to guests who were mingling near the refreshment table. He soaked up the way she looked with her hair loose, her face slightly pink from her time in the sun.

''I think Laura and I should elope.''

Jack dragged his gaze from her to give Sam his attention.

''I haven't spent more than fifteen minutes with her,'' Sam mumbled. ''Every time I try to dance with her, one of our local fellows cuts in.''

Jack grinned in response to Sam's good-natured complaints. ''Competition?''

''Don't get me wrong. I can handle it,'' Sam said with confidence.

Jack laughed with him. A first, he realized. So did Sam. Uncertainty crept into the older man's eyes. Jack couldn't blame him for wondering what the hell had just happened. He was as confused as Sam, who sent him another hesitant grin. How much of what Abby was making him feel had gentled his anger? For nearly a decade he and Sam had shared polite conversation, especially in public. But never a laugh.

"Guess I'll go dance with my love." Sam took a step, then swiveled a look over his shoulder. "What about you?"

His love? Both amused and amazed, Jack stared at his father's back. He hadn't known Sam possessed a romantic bone in his body. Regardless, the idea of a dance worked for him.

He closed the distance to Abby, and noticed that once more she was glancing in her son's direction. Austin had wandered only feet from where a mule for the kids to pet was tied to a railing. "I've never seen a kid who likes animals as much as he does."

She'd known he was near before he'd spoken, before his hand warmed her waist. "Every free moment he has he hangs around the stables," she said with a smile. She saw Austin and Chris talking to another boy, who Abby thought was called Kevin.

"Come on." Jack took her hand and drew her with him toward the dancers. "Dance with me."

It occurred to her that she probably looked calm, but she was suddenly a bundle of nerves as he brought her into his arms. Romantic music, soft lights, bodies intimate. A dangerous combination, Abby thought. "It's been a long time since I've danced."

His eyes never leaving hers, Jack slid his hand from her back to the curve of her waist. She felt wonderful. Smelled wonderful. Her eyes looked darker, shining in the dim light. He wanted to feel the velvety softness of her flesh, taste her sweetness. He wanted this woman in his life again.

Abby tilted her head back, stared at his smiling lips. "I've heard people never forget how to ride bikes." With his mouth so close, memories of hot kisses closed in on her. "Or horses?"

He would have liked to bring her tighter against him, feel the softness that had been so familiar to him years ago. "Or how to dance?"

There was such a temptation to close her eyes. "Or how to dance," she repeated. Relaxing with him, her cheek pressed to his, she let the soft music lull her and concentrated on the steady beat of his heart against her. She was aching for another kiss, for his touch, for another night, another memory.

Lost in her thoughts, it took a second for her mind to register that the music had changed to a more upbeat tempo. She started to pull away.

Jack let her get an arm's length from him, then he twirled her around. Laughing, they danced to the quick-paced number the way they'd done so often years ago. When the music slowed again, he didn't let go, and they were close once more, swaying to the lulling, romantic tune.

Time seemed to stop. Abby could have been that young girl again full of dreams, believing the handsome cowboy holding her would never let her go. But she couldn't go back, she tried to remind herself. She'd changed.

As a reminder of all that was different, she looked over Jack's shoulder in Austin's direction. A second passed, then another while she scanned the area for him. "Jack?"

In less time than it took to grab a breath, he heard panic rise in her voice and pulled back to look at her.

Her heart picking up speed, Abby broke from him and rushed around people to reach the boy she'd seen Austin talking to. "Kevin, where's Austin?" she asked.

"Easy, Abby." Jack was right beside her.

"Him and Chris went out there," the boy said.

Abby's heart hammered as Kevin pointed behind him at the darkness of the desert.

"Why would they go out there?" she asked, looking into the inky blackness.

"Austin said he saw a dog."

No dog would be wandering in the desert. "A coyote?" She shot a look at Jack. "That's what he saw, isn't it?"

Jack placed an arm around her shoulder, tried to keep her panic at bay. "We don't know that. It might have been a neighbor's dog. They can't have gone far, Abby."

Nearby, Chris's mother appeared to sway back against her husband as she death-gripped his arm. Jack noticed Sam offering them reassuring words about the boys' safety.

"What if the coyote—" Abby couldn't utter the words. "He's fine. You're right. They're both fine."

Jack kept her tight to him for a long moment. "I'll find them." He turned to Guy, who'd joined them. ''You go out that way,'' he said, motioning. ''I doubt that they've wandered far from the lights.''

Sam touched Abby's arm. ''We'll spread out. We'll find them.''

''He wants a dog so badly,'' she said to her aunt who had taken Jack's position beside Abby.

''Let's sit over there,'' Laura urged, indicating a bench nearby.

''I can't sit. I have to go with them. I have to look for Austin,'' she insisted as she watched the lights of lanterns and flashlights brightening the darkness of the desert, as she heard voices calling out the boys' names.

''Abby, they couldn't have gone far,'' Laura insisted.

Lantern lights swayed with movement, growing smaller while the men searching distanced themselves from the ranch.

Ray stood near, holding Jodi tightly in his arms. ''Don't be fretting too much, Abby. They left only a few minutes ago.''

Abby knew he was offering her words to comfort. He was right, she reminded herself. It wasn't as if the boys had been gone for hours. But only feet away, they could find danger. Don't do this to yourself, she insisted. Austin knew the rules, he wouldn't wander far away. He'd stay close enough to see the lights of the buildings. That sounded logical, but he was seven, and if he believed an animal needed him, he'd be thinking with his heart, not his head.

''Found them,'' someone yelled from far off.

Abby pulled away from Laura, then froze as she heard more shouts, alarmed ones, a few curses, people bellowing, "Don't move."

Unable to stand by and do nothing, she rushed forward, only to have Sam stop her from running into the darkness.

A masculine voice, Jack's, Abby thought, yelled. "Austin, stand still."

The command slithered a chill of fear down her spine. Abby gripped Sam's arm. "Oh my God, Sam." She knew without an explanation. Snakes surfaced during the cool of night.

"Guy, get a stick," Jack called out.

A few more curses, and then, "Are you ready?" She heard someone yell, "Look out."

"Got it." Again the voice sounded like Jack's.

Even as her legs went weak with relief, Abby broke free from Sam. Running forward, she hurried toward the voice, toward the flashlights. "Oh, Austin."

She saw Jack had him in his arms. He was safe. Though her arms weren't around him, Jack's were. In that instant, a realization floated over her. No one else holding her son would have given her such peace of mind. Her heart pounding, she ran to them.

He probably was holding the boy too tightly, Jack guessed. But when he'd seen the snake in striking distance of the boy's foot, he'd felt a fear rise within him that he'd never known before. He pressed his face close to Austin's for a second, then, seeing Abby, he set the boy down.

"Mom, Mom!" The threat of tears cracked his young voice.

Abby dropped to her knees and caught him to her. "Oh, Austin."

He wrapped his arms around her neck in a stranglehold. "Mom, there was a snake."

"I know." She felt him tremble. "I know." She kissed his cheek, his forehead, his cheek again. She could barely contain the need to squeeze him. "Austin, what were you doing out here?"

"I'm sorry, Mom." His arms loosened their grip slightly. "We didn't mean to go out so far." Drawing back, she saw frown lines, so unnatural on his face, marring his forehead. "Are you mad?"

"I wasn't mad, I was worried." She kissed his cheek, pressed her temple to his.

"I wanted to get the dog," he said as an explanation. "I thought he was lost."

Beside her, she heard Chris gulping words. "Then it howled," he said in a voice edged by fright.

Abby clung to Austin beyond what he was probably comfortable with, but she needed to hold him close. "It was a coyote, not a dog."

"We know." Austin's eyes appeared wider suddenly. "But I thought it was a dog. We turned around to go back, then we saw the snake."

Abby checked her imagination, not allowing herself to visualize what might have happened if Jack hadn't found the boys in time. Still, tears smarted her eyes.

Standing nearby, Jack saw her release a shaky

breath, one that indicated she was on the edge of tears. "Hey, Austin." He looked for a way to distract the boy. "Hop aboard. I'll give you a ride back to the lodge."

Tears of relief smarting her eyes, Abby averted her face from her son's stare before Jack lifted him to his shoulders. "You go ahead," she urged so Austin wouldn't see her cry. "I need to talk to Chris's mother."

"Mom's crying," Austin said low in Jack's ear.

The shakiness in her voice had given her away. Jack figured the truth was the best way to handle the moment. "Moms get scared, too."

"I didn't mean to scare her."

"She knows that," he reassured him. "But don't do that again."

"No, sir."

Through sheer willpower, Abby kept the tears from flowing. But even though more in control, she felt a knot constrict her throat and grabbed several calming breaths before she caught up with them. "I want you to rest now," she said to Austin.

"Aw, Mom, I'm okay."

Jack thought a little levity might help. "He's okay, Mom."

Abby knew that teasing tone and played along. "Don't be helpful," she said in a pseudochiding tone. Austin giggled that Jack was getting reprimanded instead of him. "You two think this is funny?" she asked, playing the stern adult to the hilt.

His eyes dancing with amusement, Austin muffled another giggle against the top of Jack's head.

"Not us," Jack answered for both of them.

"And then the emperor from Xania zapped Captain Cosmo," Austin was telling Jack while Abby unlocked the door to their rooms.

"I saw that one," Jack said about the television program meant for ten-year-olds. He'd watched it. He'd had nothing else to do. It had been nine in the morning. He'd been stuck in a hotel room in a strange city with nowhere to go, and his television choices had been limited. From the corner of his eye, he caught Abby's I-don't-believe-this expression. "I was in San Antonio, waiting to leave for a date with a mean-spirited bull," he said as a reason. "It was watch that or a cooking show."

"And *Captain Cosmo* won?"

"Only because the cooking show was a rerun, and I'd learned how to cook Cajun chicken three weeks earlier when I was in Sioux Falls."

"I got Captain Cosmo pj's," Austin said proudly. "Want to see them?"

Jack went along. The pajamas didn't interest him, but for that smile on Austin's face, he would agree to anything. It occurred to him that he was as much a sucker for the boy as he was for his mother.

"You don't have to," Abby said, to let him off the hook.

"He wants to see them, Mom," Austin insisted. "Don't you?"

"That's right," Jack said easily.

Whether he really wanted to or not, clearly he did want to please Austin. Abby moved into the adjoining room and started to pick up one of Austin's puzzles near the sofa. Unexpectedly, the laughter of father and son resounded on the air. Oh, God. She sank to a cushion as pressure filled her chest. She hadn't lied to Jack. She'd done worse. She'd stolen years of moments like that from him.

"He's getting into his pajamas," Jack said from the doorway.

"Thank you." Get a grip, Abby, she chided herself. "That was nice of you."

"What was?" Jack came around the other side of the sofa and settled beside her.

"Acting as if you wanted to see his pajamas."

"No big deal."

"To him, it was. Captain Cosmo is his hero."

Jack stared down at her delicate hands gripped tightly together. She'd had a tough evening. "I gathered that." Not knowing what he could do to help, he placed a hand over hers. "He told me he has a poster of him."

Abby leaned back against the cushion, willing herself to relax. All that had happened was over. Austin was safe. "It was a miracle of miracles that I got it for him." She talked to keep her mind free of images, of a snake, of her frightened son. "When the posters first came out, they were the hot item. I knew how much he wanted one, so I hired a baby-sitter and ran around to ten different stores before I found one.''

Jack stretched out an arm behind her on the sofa. ''He's lucky to have you.''

She took a moment to answer. ''I'm the lucky one.''

''Come here.'' His hands on her shoulders, Jack closed his arms around her, felt her tremble.

''I'm okay,'' Abby insisted on a deep breath, but for a moment longer, because he kept holding her, she stayed in his arms. For years, she'd basically stood alone. It was a nice feeling to lean on someone.

''Mom,'' Austin called out from the other room. ''I'm ready.''

She heard him, but it wasn't easy to break free from a cloud of longing. With Jack's comforting embrace around her, she yearned for this to be more than just a passing moment in her life.

''Abby.'' Jack felt her pulling inward again, and wanted to stop her. He'd been giving her space, and all the while he'd been aching for her. If he thought she didn't care, he would have backed off, but he'd seen passion in her eyes, felt it in her kiss. ''Have dinner with me tomorrow at the barn.'' Her fragrance taunted him to lean closer. ''You and Austin,'' he said before she refused.

Dinner. A friendly meal. Nothing more. And there would be three of them, Abby reminded herself. ''You're staying in the barn then?'' She remembered hours in the loft, in the bed.

"Yes," he answered.

"What time?" she asked Jack before she allowed herself to think about what she was doing.

Jack shrugged. He hadn't thought beyond the moment. "I'll get back to you," he said, and rose with her.

Abby released an unsteady sigh while she watched him cross the room to the door. There were no what ifs anymore about what she was feeling. Emotion hadn't snuck up on her. It had slammed against her like some electric charge and riveted her in place. It had consumed her whole being with its energy. It had warmed her soul and electrified her body with its heat.

She had no choice but to face the truth. She knew now that she'd never stopped loving him. She'd only fooled herself for all these years. But this time was different. This time she'd look for no promises.

Chapter Eight

Throughout the night, memories of what she and Jack had shared lingered in her mind. And though the next morning Abby tried to keep them tucked in the back of her mind, the memories were always there. She recalled the softness in his voice when they lay in the afterglow of lovemaking, the tenderness of his caress during the most casual embrace. She could write all that off to lust. But silly memories plagued her, too, like the evening he'd joined her in the bathtub still wearing his Stetson, or the morning when he'd returned from a drive to Phoenix to bring her rice and cashew chicken for lunch.

By midafternoon, she faced a few facts. She should have fought harder, made him believe that they belonged together. But she'd been afraid to do anything that might break the spell, end the happiness she'd found with him. So she'd gone along with whatever he'd said.

Had she been different back then, she might have made him realize that loving her wasn't a mistake. And though he might not have been in less of a rage at Sam, he might have reached for her instead of running off.

She knew the ground rules this time, didn't she? Whatever they found again wouldn't last. She could deal with that. What was worrying her, what made her hesitate, had nothing to do with her and Jack. Everything she did affected Austin. So no matter what she decided, she had to do everything in her power to keep Austin from getting hurt.

Needing a glass of iced tea, she entered the lodge kitchen. At the table, Wendy was filling small squares of netting with birdseed. Nearby, Jodi sat in her high chair, giggling as Ray played peekaboo behind his Stetson. "Who's doing the entertaining?" Abby asked lightly, eager for conversation to escape her own thoughts.

Ray chuckled and straightened, plopping his hat back on his head. "Can't resist this little one."

Wendy sent him a teasing grin. "He's the best baby-sitter in town."

"And proud of it." His smile deepened the many lines in his weathered face. "See ya, ladies." He placed a kiss on Jodi's forehead. "Including you, Princess Jodi."

Abby thought it sweet that Ray was so devoted

to his grand-niece. "He's a pretty great guy," she said to Wendy.

"One of the best," her friend replied, tying up one of the net packages.

After pouring a glass of iced tea, Abby settled in a chair across from Wendy. "You should have called me to help with these." She took a sip of her drink first, then grabbed a handful of birdseed and centered it in a square of netting. Behind her, she heard the bang of the kitchen's swinging door.

"Hey, Mom."

She should have known. Austin entered no room quietly.

"Whatcha doing?" he asked, stopping beside the table.

"We're filling these with birdseed to throw at your aunt and Sam after the ceremony," Wendy told him.

"Yeah." A look of delight flashed across his face. "Even grown-ups are going to do that?"

"Even grown-ups," Abby answered, sharing a grin with Wendy at the disbelief in his voice. "Where have you been?"

"At the stables. I told Aunt Laura I was going there. Rainbow is real pretty, isn't she, Mom? I sure wish I could have a horse."

"A horse." She managed not to laugh.

Not surprising to Abby, he was eyeing the huge cookie jar that Wendy had on the counter. "Know what, Mom?"

"What?" She set the tied package of birdseed

alongside the others that were already done, then rose from her chair to get him a glass of milk. "What kind of cookie do you want? Sugar or chocolate-chip?"

"Chocolate-chip." He was silent, uncharacteristic for him, while Abby set the glass and a plate of cookies before him. "Mrs. Feilder is having a camp-out," he said.

Abby recalled that Mrs. Feilder was a retired schoolteacher who'd chosen to abandon city living for a life on the ranch. She was now supervising the children's activities.

It was on the tip of Abby's tongue to tell Austin he couldn't go. Though she had confidence in the ranch employees supervising the children's program, images of scorpions and snakes and coyotes flashed through her mind.

"I can go. Right, Mom?" he asked between bites of cookie.

She wrestled to get the words out. After that jaunt he took into the desert yesterday, letting him out of her sight for even ten minutes was proving more difficult than she'd expected. "Austin—"

"Mom." He clutched her right arm. "Mom, don't say no. Everyone will think I'm a baby if they all go and I don't."

"A lot of the others won't go." The image of a fragile nine-year-old blond girl, a guest at the ranch, who lived on Park Avenue and whose mother considered a day at the zoo roughing it, flashed into Abby's mind. "Not everyone will go."

A whine entered his voice. "Mom."

"Austin, I'm not letting you camp out there," she said firmly with a sweep of her arm toward the desert.

"Not out there, Mom. Out back."

"Out back where?"

"Out back by the pavilion."

Of course, the ranch wouldn't take such young children anywhere that might be dangerous for them.

"Mom, can I? Can I?"

It wouldn't really be any different than camping out in a backyard, she reasoned. Before the protective streak rose again within her, she gave her okay. "Yes, you can."

"All right!" Austin jumped a foot in the air, sending his chair rocking. Grabbing it, he shot a look over his shoulder at Wendy. "Sorry." In response, she gave him a dismissive wave of her hand. "I'm going to go tell Chris. Okay, Mom?" he asked with such excitement, he was dancing from one foot to the other.

"Go," she said with a laugh. She doubted he heard her as he flew from the room to find his new friend.

Wendy gestured to a corner of the kitchen near the swinging door. "I'm glad you said yes."

Setting the empty milk glass and plate in the sink, Abby noted that Wendy was pointing to Austin's bulging backpack.

"He's obviously been packed since four o'clock,

even though the camp-out doesn't start until six-thirty,'' Wendy said wryly.

''Would you say he has his mother expertly wound around his finger?''

''I'd say that he has a loving mom who wants to see him happy, and do what's best for him.'' A wistfulness entered Wendy's voice. ''But sometimes it's difficult to know what's best, isn't it?''

Abby didn't pry, for Wendy didn't seem inclined to share her thoughts. She helped until they'd done enough birdseed packages so each guest had one, then went out the back door to find Mrs. Feilder and ask if Abby needed to furnish anything for the camp-out. As the door swung closed behind her, she saw Jack standing at the bottom step.

He started to climb the steps to her, when Austin and three other boys raced past them and down a path toward the pavilion. It was then Abby realized that this evening would be their first away from each other.

Anything Jack planned to say was forgotten as he saw sadness sweep across her face. ''Something wrong?''

''I'm being silly.'' Seeing his questioning look, she offered an explanation. ''Austin is going on the camp-out tonight.''

''It's safe.'' He climbed the steps to her, stopping one below her. ''They'll be in tents.''

''I'm sure it is safe. We've just never been away from each other before.''

''And…?''

"And *I* seem to be the one who's having a hard time with this new experience."

Jack couldn't exactly understand what she was feeling, but last night, when he'd been looking for Austin in the desert, he'd felt fear for another person unlike any he'd ever known. So, in a way, he understood what he viewed as an overwhelming need to protect a child. "Being a parent isn't easy."

"No, it isn't," she finally answered. In some small way she wanted Jack to know what he'd missed not being with Austin. "But it's worth whatever it takes."

Jack felt an unexpected pang of annoyance and jealousy. Some other man had given Abby that joy.

She sent him a wry, embarrassed smile. "I know I'm being silly about this."

"You're loving." Gently he touched her face. "You always were."

"That's called mushy."

He laughed easily. "Mushy?"

"Sentimental."

He would call her responsive. Compassionate. Sensitive. She had a gentle soul. So did the boy, Jack had learned.

Behind them, the back door squeaked open. "Oh, good, I caught you," Wendy said. "I counted the birdseed packages. We're short. Do you know where Laura bought the ribbon? I'll need more, and I want to match it."

"I'll find out," Abby told her.

"Uh, no, you don't have to—" Wendy grimaced

as she noticed Jack standing there, her eyes apologetic. "I didn't mean to bother you."

"I'm supposed to be checking a fence," Jack said to a retreating Wendy.

As the back door closed, Abby smiled. "She'll be apologizing for the next half hour."

"I do have to go," he said. "I'll see you—" He stopped. "Are you still coming for dinner?"

Dinner. Just the two of them. With Austin not there, they wouldn't be having a casual, not-too-cozy dinner for three. He watched her. Waited.

"You're killing my ego, Abby." Pride demanded he keep his words light. "Quit hesitating."

She stared at his mouth and wasn't able to think about anything but the pleasure she knew she'd find in another kiss. For days she'd wanted to resist more contact with him. She'd wanted to believe she didn't feel the same for him anymore. Then last night she'd accepted that she'd always loved him. "I'll come as soon as Austin's settled for the evening."

"Good. You can fry the potatoes."

Abby shared a smile with him. "Do you need me to bring anything?"

Unable to resist, he let his knuckles skim her cheek. "Just you."

Just you. Those words had spiraled a nice warm thrill right down to the tips of Abby's toes. And made her nervous.

A shower should have helped. But soaking under the spray of the water, though relaxing, didn't make her feel any more certain she was doing the right thing tonight.

For a longer time than necessary, she brushed her teeth. It was logical that she was edgy. Stepping into Jack's place would flood her with memories.

During those summer months, she'd cooked meals with him in the tiny kitchen in the barn, sat on the sofa watching television and eating popcorn, spent nights with him in the queen-size bed with its patchwork quilt.

So tonight she'd have dinner with him in the small kitchen as she'd done many times. And then? Don't wonder. Just go, she told herself. For one night, she wasn't going to listen to good sense. For one night, she wanted to be that young girl again; she wanted to follow her heart.

Strolling up a hill several hundred feet away from the lodge, Abby looked up at Sam's home. It was a lovely white, two-story farmhouse with several eaves. Abby recalled sitting on Sam's porch swing with Jack. Soon her aunt would live in that home with its bright yellow kitchen and enormous windows.

A gentle breeze whipped around her as she walked past the house, then climbed an incline toward the working part of the ranch. Besides the house, there were sheds, the bunkhouse, the ranch hands' stable and corral. Set higher on a hill was the converted gray barn—Jack's place.

Abby eyed the front door. Jack could hurt her. There was so much risk in reaching out to him. And so much to lose if she didn't. Before she had time to consider, she rapped on the door.

He'd needed to see her here again, Jack realized the instant he opened the door. When she stepped inside, he felt pleasure.

And he felt nervous. He'd rushed around earlier picking up clothes, dirty dishes and this morning's newspaper. He'd started dinner, then taken a shower. And he'd warned himself not to expect too much tonight. But damn, the need to touch her clawed at him.

"Still like margaritas?" he asked. Her eyes looked dark to him, vulnerable, and a touch uncertain. "Or do you want a soda?"

"Still do," she answered. Nothing was feeling steady, not even her breathing. "But I'll have a soda."

The home was so unique. The huge room was as she remembered, still sparsely decorated. Most of the furnishings were discards from guest quarters, a lamp, tables, a beige sofa and chair. She crossed the plank floor to a staircase that led to the loft, to the bedroom. She'd loved the view of distant mountains from the loft. She'd loved being in his home. "You've changed nothing."

Jack dropped ice cubes into a glass. He couldn't think about anything but how soft she looked, how right it seemed to have her here with him. "No reason to."

Abby stepped toward the kitchen. "I thought I was going to do the potatoes," she said as she saw them browning in a frying pan beside the pork chops.

"You're a guest tonight." He went to move the frying pan and winced when he grabbed the hot handle.

Without thinking, Abby reached into a drawer for a pot holder. "Are you okay?"

"Fine."

Déjà vu slipped over her. They'd stood in almost the same place on another night. As she'd stretched for something, a plate, she remembered now, he'd slipped his arms around her. Dinner had been forgotten that night. "Here." She set the pot holder on the counter near him. Maybe this hadn't been a good idea.

Jack turned around. Standing tense, her back straight, she looked ready to run. All that hadn't been said stood between them. "Abby, what happened wasn't about you and me. You know that now, don't you?"

She didn't want to talk, to relive that night. She simply wanted to forget all that had gone wrong, because all the I'm sorrys in the world wouldn't explain how he could have hurt her like that.

Jack read her well. Her lips thinned. She wouldn't meet his eyes. She was gathering her defenses. Even if he restirred all the hurt he'd inflicted on her before, he needed to tell her more. "I wasn't thinking straight that night." Possibly she wouldn't understand. But no matter what did or didn't happen between them, he wanted her to know the truth. "I was angry after talking to my father.'' An understatement. He'd been furious. After that argument with his father, what he'd needed most was her softness, her tender caress, and he hadn't realized that until it was too late.

Slowly she faced him, surprised by his words, because she'd been expecting him to utter some excuse. She remembered that he'd promised to meet her by the pavilion. She'd waited almost an hour then had gone to the lodge to find him.

Jack switched off the burners. ''That night, I went to Sam's office to get a bill of sale for Willow, the chestnut mare.'' He leaned against the stove. ''I couldn't find the paper in his desk. I knew the combination to the safe, but I'd never had reason to open it until then. I thought Sam had put the paper for the horse there, so I riffled through some documents.'' He paused for a second. He no longer felt anger. Over the years, he'd become numb to all the feelings—the disbelief, the disappointment, mostly the hurt. ''I found divorce papers,'' he finally said. ''Sam's and my mother's.''

It took a full moment for Abby to register what those words meant. ''I don't understand. Your mother died in childbirth.''

''That's what I'd believed. That's what Sam had told me. For twenty-three years, I believed a lie. I thought she died when I was born.''

And had carried unnecessary guilt with him, Abby knew. What had Sam done? And why? Abby bridged the inches between them. Why would he put his son through such pain? ''Jack, what did Sam say?''

''What could he say? He'd lied. She'd never died having me. He'd divorced her.''

Abby took care with her words. ''Sam told you that?''

''I didn't want to hear his explanation. But he claimed she left because she wanted a dancing career. I didn't care to know what ended the marriage.''

She imagined his pain as if it had just happened. If only she'd been with him. How much he must have hurt to learn that the man he'd loved, idolized, had deceived him. ''Jack, I don't understand this. Why would Sam do that?''

Hadn't he asked the same question dozens of times? There was no logical answer as far as he was concerned. ''Who knows? You tell me why someone who claimed he loved me would lie to me, let me believe that I was responsible for my mother's death?''

''I don't think he wanted you to feel that way,'' she said in Sam's defense, recalling the loving father Sam had been. In fact, she wasn't sure Sam ever knew that was what Jack had felt.

He started to step around her, but her hand closed over his. ''I know what you're going to say.'' He stood still, close to her now. ''It wasn't my fault, but you know—dammit, you know, I always thought he lost her because of me.''

And he wouldn't risk any woman's life the same

way. Yes, she remembered. That was why he'd insisted on no strings, no commitment between them. He'd wanted no children, never wanted to feel responsible for another woman's death. So much of what went wrong between them had been because of what he'd believed about his mother, because of the lie his father had told.

Weariness crept into his voice. "I loved you." Jack wanted her to know that. "But I'd convinced myself that I couldn't give you anything permanent. Because of his lie, I never asked you to go with me."

Abby pressed her palm against his cheek. She couldn't speak. They should have never lost each other. Why had Sam done that? Don't go there, she warned herself. How could she judge Sam for what he'd done when she'd deceived Jack, too?

"I left that night to find her," he said.

"Your mother?" With his nod, her heart twisted.

"I really wasn't thinking straight," he stated. "All I knew was that I wanted to get away from him—as fast as I could."

If only she hadn't left the next morning. She would have been there for his phone call. "Did you ever find her?"

"Before I left, I got him to tell me where he'd thought she'd gone. So I drove all night to L.A."

Abby could only imagine the harsh words, the hurt that had passed between the two men that night.

"I was supposed to be in a rodeo in Montana a week from then. But I went to Los Angeles. It took time to trace her. The only person I found with her maiden name was an aunt I'd never known I had. She wasn't thrilled to see me. It seems my mother never mentioned she'd been married. And I guess my mother had hit her for some money, and never paid it back. But my aunt told me that she'd died in a car accident. So that was that. I headed for Montana.'' He finally met her stare again. ''She never pursued a dancing career. My aunt hadn't even known she wanted one. I wondered then why they'd really divorced. I wondered if Sam had lied about that, too.''

Never before had she wanted so much to wrap her arms around someone. ''I don't know what to say.''

''There's nothing to say. For three years I didn't come back here. I didn't want to see him. I lived on the road, going from rodeo to rodeo. But hell, I couldn't cut him out of my life. I realized I might never understand why he kept the truth from me, but staying away didn't change what had happened.''

He stretched for a breath. ''One Christmas I came home. We talked, Sam apologized. I assumed he'd deceived me because she'd hurt his pride by leaving him. So instead of telling me the truth, he made up a story to save face.''

Abby mulled over all he'd said. It occurred to her that he would never have been hers. Though he no longer dealt with the emotional baggage of causing his mother's death, for another reason, he would never give her what she wanted. He didn't trust Sam anymore, might never again. And he wouldn't help with the ranch. All the facts added up to the same conclusion. He wouldn't settle down now any more than he would have before.

"I missed you, Abby, but I couldn't give you the life you wanted," he said. What could he have offered her? A life of chasing rodeos? She'd told him that she hated the constant moving, leaving friends when she'd been a child. Never being able to call anyplace home. He knew that's what she wanted most. It was what she would still want.

Silently Abby inched closer to him. She'd needed him so badly back then when she'd been pregnant, working nights and trying to finish school. Ironically, he'd needed her just as much, only he hadn't realized that.

Love controlled her. Sliding her arms around his waist, she stood close for a long moment, her cheek pressed to his as she longed to give him all the comfort she hadn't been able to offer eight years ago.

Tenderly, Jack framed her face with his hands. He kissed her cheek, the tip of her nose, an eyelid.

Even if she could have only one more night with him, she wanted it. She ran a hand over the back of his head. Wasn't his love what she'd craved all this time? It's always been only you, she wanted to say.

Jack saw what he longed for—desire in her dark eyes, the invitation in her parted lips. He wanted to take her, rush her. Instead, he slowly let his fingers move down the buttons of her blouse. She deserved better from him. She deserved gentleness. He searched her face while he pushed her shirt aside, let it slither to the floor. His fingers, more unsteady than he'd expected, touched the silk of her camisole, and all he could think about was the flesh beneath it. "Come with me." He caught her hand, led her toward the stairs.

At the bottom of the steps, he kissed her again, long, thoroughly, a man dying of thirst. She'd always been the only one for him. It had been her face haunting him, her touch he'd craved all these years. With her mouth clinging to his, he gathered her in his arms.

Abby knew they traveled the staircase that led to the loft. She knew when they entered the bedroom. She felt herself floating before she sank into the mattress. With his mouth on hers, dreams sprang alive again, and she pushed aside any niggling concerns. All that mattered was the moment. He murmured something. She didn't need soft words. She sought his taste, his tongue, the warm recesses of his mouth. She only wanted the lips on hers that were moving slowly, stirring an ache through her.

She yanked at his shirt, freeing it from the band at his waist, and slid her hands under the cloth, splaying her fingers to feel as much of the muscles and the smoothness as she could.

Lifting first one shoulder and then the other, she helped him slide her camisole down. She heard the thunder of her own heart, the softness of his voice as it enticed and urged. Together they shoved down her jeans while their lips clung. Memories spun around her, memories once shared, memories about to begin.

She didn't speak. She could barely think, his every caress binding them together again. A wanting she never thought she'd feel again consumed her as he hooked his fingers into her panties. She was wild beneath his hands, beneath his mouth, as he traced a slow, sensuous trail across her belly. When he slipped the last wisp of silk from her, a breathtaking urgency rushed fast and furious through her.

In the moonlit room, with the coolness of the evening caressing her skin, she wanted to capture every second of every night in a single one. She watched him, standing beside the bed now, shrugging clothes from himself, and all the emotion she thought she'd never feel again closed in on her. An eternity passed while he reached for the foil package. Then he came near again. In the shadowy room, his eyes were intense, exciting. She opened her arms to him, welcoming the hard strength of him against her.

Heat. Excitement. They spiraled through her. For too long she'd lived on memories. Now there was no yesterday. Maybe there would be no tomorrow for them, either. But if only for this moment, she wanted him to know she was his. She couldn't— wouldn't—worry about tomorrow. It was too far away.

Jack rolled her with him. Blood pounding in his head, he filled himself with her, with her taste, and her sweetness. But as her fingers grazed his hip, she took control.

A brush of her fingertip, a stroke that turned swifter, and like an inescapable force, desire took possession of him. He rode an edge of control until he thought he'd explode with it.

He drew her to him and her slender legs wrapped around him, urged him closer. His heart beating harder, he buried his face in the curve of her neck, and as she opened her body to him, he entered her. She arched against him and called his name. He'd longed for her, had ached to make her breathless like this. But he'd forgotten the madness she could soar him toward, the breath she could snatch from him. She was seductive, enticing, exotic.

Losing himself in the moment, he heard only her moans. They played in his head along with the hammering of his own pulse. Only she existed. Only she mattered. He gripped her hips, then on a muffled moan, he took her with him, letting the madness, the stunning madness, slip over them.

Chapter Nine

"Are you awake?" Abby murmured, opening her eyes to the gray light of dawn. Languid, tired, she wanted to stay beside him all day. Lightly she stroked the faint line of hair down his belly. How was it possible they could find so much again? It was as if they'd never been apart. They'd moved as one, anticipating the wants and desires of the other. They'd fit perfectly.

"I'm awake."

She angled her head to look up at him and saw his eyes were still shut. Just as content, she nuzzled against him for a moment longer, lightly running fingertips down his lean ribs.

Sunlight cast the room in a warm golden glow. A rustic room, the bedroom contained a wall filled with bookshelves. He had eclectic taste, enjoying everything from autobiographies to western paperbacks. This was a side of him few people knew. Beneath the macho-cowboy image was an intellect. A Civil War buff, he could discuss not only battle sites, but also the strategies used by Lee and Grant during skirmishes. During the past year, she'd noticed that, like him, Austin had a tendency to become intense, learning everything he could about something that caught his interest.

In their son's case, his fascination was with Captain Cosmo. Austin had collected coloring books, comic books, posters and action figures of the superhero.

Unlike either of them, Abby collected nothing. It was a trait learned early in life. There had been no point in saving anything. Because she and her mother moved often, they traveled light. Possessions weren't a part of their lives.

"Who's making breakfast?" Jack asked, his voice slightly hoarse.

Abby shifted and kissed his chest. "If you make coffee, I'll make breakfast."

"Sounds like a deal." Jack eased to his side and propped himself on an elbow. She looked sweet and young with her hair mussed from sleep, her face clean of makeup. Absently he toyed with a strand of her hair. "You're beautiful."

How easily he could make her believe in them again, she reflected. Letting her head drop back to the pillow, she gave his mouth freedom to explore her throat, and she shut her eyes. With the caress of his lips, she concentrated on sensations that the silent moment offered—the heat and hardness of him against her, the sound of his breathing, the sensitive touch of his strong hand roaming over her breast. "You weaken me," she admitted softly. "I wish— I wish we could stay here all day."

"We did that once," Jack murmured in a slow lazy manner close to her ear. He wanted to stir the warmth between them again. He wanted her to feel everything in the brightness of daylight.

Abby smiled with the memory he'd aroused about the camping trip they'd taken. For four days, they'd been alone, and had spent most of it making love. "That was such a wonderful time." It was also when she'd gotten pregnant. Austin had been a child of love.

He skimmed the soft roundness of her hip. "We have a few more hours."

She really wanted to stay, not think about anything except how wonderful it felt to be beside him. "Never being satisfied is supposed to be good for the soul." But what if Austin, for some reason, looked for her early this morning?

"Who says?" he mumbled in a husky morning voice.

As he molded her to him, she felt her body swell with the need for him again. "Me," she said on a sigh. "This—" She heaved a breath. "I can't do this. I need to go." She laughed, and before she lost the will to leave his embrace, she shoved him to his back. Kneeling beside him, she bent forward and kissed smiling lips. "It's comforting to know that you'll be as miserable as I will," she murmured against his mouth.

More, Jack mused. "Possibly."

"Possibly?" Drawing back, Abby saw his grin and jabbed his ribs lightly. "Possibly?" she mocked again, then pushed at his chest to move away. "Don't even try to deny it." When he made a grab for her, she scrambled from the bed. "Beat you to the shower." Behind her, she heard the mattress springs squeak as he bounded from it. When she was a few steps from the bathroom door, he fell in place beside her.

"Sure you'll beat me." He gave her an ungentlemanly shove with his shoulder to step in front of her.

"I'm first," Abby yelled at his bare backside. Trailing him, she laughed as he disappeared into the bathroom. By the time she reached it, water was running. "You cheat," she insisted, and flung back the shower curtain. As an arm snaked around her waist and lifted her off her feet, she squealed.

"I know," Jack mumbled. With water rushing over them, he pressed her against the wet wall of the shower and closed his mouth over hers once more.

Abby realized that she'd never expected a morning like this again. In the bathroom, drying her hair, she listened to Jack in the other room whistling

''When a Man Loves a Woman.'' The sound grew softer, indicating he'd left the room and was on his way down the stairs.

As she clicked the switch to turn off the hair dryer, the silence around her forced thoughts on her that she'd been dodging. She wanted to tell him the truth. She wanted them to put the past behind them. But she kept imagining the moment, Jack's shock, his anger, his disgust with her for keeping such a secret. And she wanted a little longer.

As she wandered down the stairs from the loft, she saw him on a stool near a wall of windows. He didn't look up from the sheet of paper he was reading. In passing, Abby saw one word. *Entrant*. Was he already preparing for another rodeo? Last night she'd traced the scars he'd collected since he'd begun following the rodeo, the one along his rib cage, another on his forearm, and the most recent one stretching from midthigh to his kneecap. All reminders of what she wanted to forget. He had a life that she and Austin couldn't be a part of.

That wasn't easy to remember. Because she was here? she wondered. Hadn't she known this was the danger in coming here?

Standing in the middle of the kitchen with everything where it used to be, she felt as if eight years had never passed.

She moved to the coffeemaker, which was hissing now. Jack had dumped last night's dinner before she'd come downstairs. If she was hungry this morning, he must be starving.

A quick check of the refrigerator revealed necessities to start the day—eggs, milk, butter, even bacon. Abby quickly whisked eggs, and had them cooking in a pan when he moseyed in.

"Want anything else for that?" he asked, gesturing toward the omelette she was making.

"Cheese."

"You know, I'd forgotten how loudly you snore."

Abby paused in moving the spatula through the eggs in the frying pan and swiveled a look over her shoulder to see him shrugging into his shirt. "Excuse me, but I *don't* snore."

He thought that she looked adorable. Her hair tousled, she stood before him in one of his shirts, the sleeves rolled up into bulky cuffs. "I told you before that you did." Jack opened the refrigerator and bent forward to hide his smile. "I've got an onion but no tomatoes."

She heard the trace of humor in his voice, and didn't rise to the bait again. "Cheese?" she repeated.

"No cheese." Watching her moving around the kitchen was almost painful. She'd leave first this time, he knew. And forever, whenever he stepped into this room, he'd see her standing there.

Satisfied at the way the omelette looked, Abby slid it from the pan to a plate. "Breakfast is ready."

Behind her now, Jack slipped a hand across the front of her waist. He'd dreamed of a moment like this. "I'm crazy about you."

With all she'd longed for within her reach, she could almost believe, Abby realized. Turning in his arms, she smiled, kissed a corner of his lips. For right now, this had to be enough. "I'm crazy about you, too."

"You always did know how to start the day."

With you. Only you. "Here." Abby handed him a plate.

Appreciatively, Jack eyed the fluffy eggs. "You also make one hell of a great-looking breakfast."

"Thank you." She followed him to the table. "I don't get a chance to do this often. Austin hates eggs."

Jack set down his plate, then crossed to the coffeemaker when it released a final hiss. "A cereal man, huh?"

Abby turned back to the counter to retrieve napkins. "Pancakes."

"He's a great kid, Abby. I like him." More than once when he'd been in a foul mood, Austin had come up to him, and with a few words from the boy, or with one of his questions, he'd made Jack smile.

At the counter, Abby stilled. Those were words that meant far more to her than he'd ever know. She couldn't help wondering if fatherhood might make a difference to him. Perhaps he would change his life for Austin. But what if he wouldn't? Austin would gain a father in name only. One who might remember to send him a birthday card, maybe even visit with him a couple of weeks a year. She couldn't bear to see her son's heart broken.

"He told me that he likes to ski, but only went once with you." Jack returned to the table as she did. Beneath the morning sunlight, her hair had a rich reddish tone. "When did you learn?"

"I haven't." After placing napkins by their plates, she settled on a nearby chair. "Thank you," she said about the cup he set before her. The scent of coffee drifted up to her. "We were both on the bunny hill. We might go again this winter." Where would he be then? she wondered, and felt an unsettled sensation in the vicinity of her heart as she experienced the first hint of what she'd feel without him. "Are you entered in a rodeo after the wedding?"

Cautiously, Jack sipped the steaming brew in his cup. "I've been off the circuit because of the injury."

"And eager to get back?"

"What else would I do?"

Abby knew it wasn't a question he expected her response to. While she stood at the sink later, her hands in the sudsy water, she accepted what hadn't been said. If he wasn't in rodeo, he would be a rancher. But because of how he now felt about Sam that would never happen.

"I'll meet you in the lobby at nine-thirty, and we can drive to the rodeo," Jack said while drying a plate.

Abby had forgotten about it. That was amazing

since Austin had talked about nothing else ever since Sam had announced the rodeo taking place. With the reminder, she left Jack to finish the dishes and rushed upstairs to dress. Anxious to go to the rodeo, Austin may have already been looking for her. It took only minutes to slip on clothes. When she returned downstairs, she saw Jack waiting outside for her.

The sound of a woodpecker, the sight of roadrunners scurrying between desert brush, the warmth of the morning sun accompanied their walk toward the lodge. Hand in hand with Jack, she felt like that young girl so full of dreams who'd been here nearly a decade ago. She'd wanted to spend the rest of her life with him. Here, at this ranch. Now, because of his estrangement from Sam, he would never ask her to do that.

"What are you daydreaming about?" Jack asked.
You. Us. "How much Austin is looking forward to today," she said, because that was partially true. She sent him a smile that she thought he was looking for, but her gaze strayed to Wendy, sitting nearby, under one of the large elms. "Something's wrong," Abby said, certain by the look on Wendy's face and her pinkish nose that she'd been crying. "I'd better go to her."

Jack squeezed her hand before releasing it. "Yeah, okay." He'd already decided to find Guy, and learn for himself what was happening. "I'll meet you later."

Not wanting to startle Wendy, Abby said nothing

with her approach and quietly dropped to the summery green grass beside her, waiting until her friend looked up. "Can I help?"

Wendy gave her hand a backhand wave as if her problem was unimportant. "It's nothing." She sighed. "No, forget that. Everything is wrong," she admitted. "Guy and I had a biggie of a fight." Annoyance instead of sadness crept into her voice. "He's twenty-nine years old. I know there are cowboys older than him, but Sam has offered him the stable manager's job, and a great salary if Guy wants to stay home. I want him to," she said adamantly.

Abby braced her back against the tree trunk. The warmth of the sun pressed down on her. "What has Guy said?"

"He'd think about it." Wendy bent her knees and wrapped her arms around them. "He told me that he'd think about it."

Abby noted that she didn't sound too hopeful. "Some of them can't get rodeo out of their blood."

"Someone like Jack, I suppose. He's one of those guys who needs danger and thrills. He likes living on that edge. That's fine for him. He isn't married, and doesn't have kids."

Abby frowned with her words.

Wendy obviously saw it. "I'm sorry, Abby. That probably wasn't what you wanted to hear."

"It's the truth." As Wendy began to stand, Abby pushed to her feet. "I know that as well as you do."

"I'm afraid so. Guy's made a decent living in rodeo, won a few titles in single events, but rodeo

isn't ever going to be for him what it is for Jack.''
As if aware she'd unwittingly drooped Abby's spirits, she offered encouragement. "Could be Jack's
ready to settle down now. That would be great for
you two.'' She gestured with her head toward Jack's
barn. "I saw you come out with him. You know, I
always thought you two were perfect for each
other.''

Looking over her shoulder, Abby brushed dried
grass from the back of her jeans until she felt she'd
reveal less when she met Wendy's stare. "I thought
the same about you two. Maybe Guy will see that
you're right.''

"I can only hope.'' Worry veed Wendy's eyebrows even though she produced a smile. "Are you
going to the rodeo?''

"We'll see you there.''

Curiosity sprang into her friend's voice. "Is we—
you and Jack?''

"And Austin.''

"See, that sounds promising,'' Wendy said a little
too brightly, as if trying hard to lift her own spirits.

With their steps closer to the lodge, Abby heard
laughter. Her gaze traveled to a corral. Several
guests were taking turns to rope a hay bale that wore
a set of plastic horns. Not feet away was her son.

His eyes looked bluer, his smile brighter. "Hi,
Wendy,'' he said first, remembering his manners.
"Mom, we had a terrific time at the camp-out.''

"That's great.'' She curled her fingers over his
shoulder to have some contact with him. "You can

tell me all about it upstairs. You need to shower now, so we can leave for the rodeo.''

''Why do I have to take a shower? It's going to be dusty.''

Abby didn't argue. She directed a look at him that silently communicated he was stretching her patience.

On a mumbled, ''Aw, Mom,'' he whipped around and climbed the stairs.

Wendy chuckled softly, then, looking more serious, she placed a hand on Abby's arm. ''Thanks for listening to me.''

It seemed like so little. Abby hugged her. ''Anytime. I hope everything goes well.''

''Me, too.'' Her voice wavered slightly, indicating her emotions were still shaky.

Feeling sad for friends, Abby went up to her room. All she could do was hope Wendy and Guy worked out their problems. While she changed into clean clothes in one room, she heard Austin in the shower, singing off-key some song she guessed he'd learned last night. The volume on the song rose right before the sound of the running water stopped.

Abby was pulling on her boots when he came out of the bathroom. Though his hair still dripped, he tugged a T-shirt over his head. She passed him and retrieved a clean towel from the bathroom.

''Here,'' she said, handing it to him after his wet head popped through the shirt opening. ''Tell me about the camp-out.''

''It was really neat, Mom.'' His eyes sparkled.

''We ate all kinds of good stuff,'' he said, draping the towel over his head. ''Like hot dogs. And we roasted marshmallows and stuck 'em between graham crackers with some chocolate candy. And they told us ghost stories.''

''Scary ones?'' She knew if they scared him a little, then the evening was a success.

''I wasn't scared.'' That meant he was, Abby knew. ''Though some of the little kids were. And this morning I helped cook breakfast.''

''You did?'' Her baby was growing up. ''What did you make?'' she asked while they descended the steps to the lobby.

''I made orange juice. I squeezed oranges into a pitcher.''

She felt motherly relief that his step toward independence was smaller than she'd originally thought. ''Hmm. I bet it was good.''

He wrinkled his nose. ''I didn't like it. It had seeds and some other stuff in it. Do you think we'll see a bull chase anybody today?''

''I hope not.''

''Jack says he had one chase him around the arena.''

Abby thought that sounded like an exaggeration.

''And did you see that scar on his arm? A horn from a bull as big as a car did that. Did you know that?''

Interested in who said what, Abby prodded, ''Did Jack tell you that?''

''No. Chris did. And his sister told him.''

Chris had a sixteen-year-old sister with a rose tattoo on her upper left breast and a tendency to tell tales filled with embellishments. "Who told her?"

"Dunno." Feet from them, he saw Chris and his family, who were waiting for the ranch shuttle that would take them to the rodeo. "Can I go over there?"

"Yes, go ahead."

Several other guests were returning from a cattle drive, and still talking, not only about the breakfast they'd had on the range but also about the beetle someone declared was big enough to saddle that had perched on the brim of a guest's cowboy hat.

Not far from everyone, lawn mowers buzzed. Abby noticed the landscaper's truck parked near one of the sheds. In preparation for the wedding, he and his crew were mowing grass and clipping shrubbery.

"It's going to look lovely, isn't it?"

Abby swung around in response to her aunt's voice. A Cheshire cat grin appeared fixed on Laura's face while she surveyed the area as if visualizing it on her wedding day, when rows of white folding chairs would line the immaculately kept grass.

"Yes, it will be," Abby answered. She'd been with her aunt at the florist's when she'd placed her order. Along with Laura's bridal bouquet and her own, the florist would bring a flowered trellis and set pots of blossoms, mostly carnations, mums and gardenias, around the swimming pool.

"Everyone is excited about going to the rodeo today."

Abby noticed the round spots of color on Laura's cheeks. Lately, she was excited about everything. One of the fringe benefits of being in love. Hadn't she thought that the sun shone brighter when she'd fallen in love with Jack?

"Austin's walk in the desert certainly provided a scare, didn't it?" Laura asked.

"Uh-huh," Abby said distractedly as Sam came close to them.

"Hello, ladies." An arm at her aunt's waist, he kissed her temple.

"We were talking about Austin going into the desert," Laura said.

Sam looked at Abby. "A scary moment for you."

Abby nodded. Just being around them made her smile. They looked so in love. It seemed as if nothing was wrong in their lives.

"There's Jack," her aunt said as he came out of a nearby supply shed.

Abby noticed the light in Sam's eyes had dulled with a sad regret when he looked Jack's way. "I should go," she said. "I'll see you both later." She moved forward to meet Jack. It seemed so wrong that the closeness he and Sam had once shared was gone.

"I missed you." To satisfy a need he'd had since leaving her this morning, Jack slipped an arm around her waist and took a quick kiss. He had missed her. That realization had hit him half an hour after leaving her. The feeling hadn't left until this moment.

Abby could have easily forgotten where they were. Her arm around his neck, her hip against his, she set a hand to his chest, felt the steady, even beat of his heart beneath her palm. "That was quite a hello." The smile starting to curl the edges of her lips weakened as she spotted Austin approaching them. It occurred to her that he'd never seen a man kiss her before.

Not bashful, her son didn't make her guess his thoughts about that for long. "He kissed you because he likes you," he informed Abby.

"Is that so?"

"Uh-huh." Austin darted a look from her to Jack and back to her. "We talked about that."

Jack looked rather smug, piquing Abby's curiosity. "And exactly what did you talk about?"

"That we both like you," her son said so matter-of-factly that her heart twisted with the deeper meaning in those words. She was also grateful for his logic. That reason obviously was a good enough reason for the kiss.

Austin rocked back on his heels in the manner of someone satisfied with life.

"Ready to go?" Jack looked from Austin to her.

"He's been ready since last week," Abby informed him.

Jack laughed and tapped the top of Austin's hat. "Then let's go."

They caught the end of the parade, then enjoyed hamburgers and french fries at a restaurant with a rustic exterior. At the fairgrounds, the scents of leather, hay and livestock mingled in the air.

Austin walked between them while they moved along with a crowd of tourists, his eyes wide as he took in the sights.

In the fenced area near the chutes, a few contestants rested on the ground, leaning back on their saddles. Others checked rigging bags or practiced lassoing while some riders used the time before competition to tape wrists, rosin some ropes or walk their horses.

Abby kept Austin close and, along with Jack, trailed the crowd to the grandstand. The music of a country band grew louder.

Fascinated with everything, Austin craned his neck to see the musicians who were performing for the spectators already seated. "Will there be clowns at the rodeo?"

Jack touched the boy's back to steer him to a VIP section near the announcer. "Always. They're important. Without them, the riders could get hurt."

"Hey, Jack," one fellow called out. A contestant's number was pinned to his back. "You signed up for the Calgary Stampede?"

"Not yet," Jack replied.

But he would, Abby assumed, recalling that the Calgary Stampede was one of the bigger rodeos. "Austin, look." Abby turned his attention to the bull being led toward a livestock pen as much to distract herself from Jack's conversation as make sure the boy saw the animal. She couldn't afford to forget what she'd found with Jack wouldn't last.

"Sit here, honey," she said to Austin, guiding him to a spot.

Before Jack joined them, he was stopped several times. Another reminder, Abby reflected. When he entered a rodeo arena, everyone knew him. This was his world.

"Mom, see that!"

She traced Austin's excited stare. In the dusty arena, clowns scurried about, entertaining the crowd while a bull banged at the wall of a nearby chute.

Jack joined them in time for the singing of the national anthem. As it finished, clowns rolled barrels into the arena.

"Going to have barrel racing, ladies and gentlemen," the announcer said. "But first, just heard we got rodeo's own Jack McShane here, folks. How about a big hand for four-time World Rodeo Champion, Jack McShane."

Standing, Jack waved his hat at the applauding and whistling crowd.

Austin gaped, awestruck. "Wow, Mom." His eyes were riveted to Jack's gleaming gold and silver buckle with the embossed words World Champion on it. It was not something he'd worn at the ranch. "Do you see his buckle, Mom?"

The child's delight carried over. With everything he watched, he burst with new enthusiasm. "She was really fast," he said about one of the women riders who'd finished racing her horse around barrels that were set in a cloverleaf fashion in the arena. "Wasn't she real fast, Jack?"

Jack had suddenly become the authority on everything.

During the next event, Austin literally sat on the edge of his seat watching the bull riding.

Jack, too, seemed tense when one contestant was announced. Leaning forward, his arms braced on his thighs and his hands clutched, he never took his eyes from the arena.

When the gate opened, the bull charged forward. Clinging to the rope, the young-looking contestant struggled against the animal arching and bucking. Veering left, then right, the bull tossed him. His head lowering, the animal spun around and charged. The crowd gasped. While the rider scrambled to his feet, a clown danced before the bull, dodging the horns long enough to let the rider escape.

Abby waited until the rider reached the safety of the fence before she satisfied her curiosity. "Do you know him?"

Over Austin's head, Jack met her stare. "I know his dad better. The kid's just out of Junior Rodeo. Bet his dad's chewing off his fingertips."

Abby understood. Young, inexperienced, the boy could make a tragic mistake. "How old is he?"

"Sixteen."

Abby scowled. In nine years, Austin could do that. She mentally shuddered, unable to imagine being the mother who was watching her child risking injury for eight seconds of fame, a silver buckle and prize money.

"You did *all* this?" Austin regarded him with a look of wonder.

Abby had an overflowing scrapbook as a record of Jack's whole career. "He won them all," she was quick to remind Austin. If Austin was going to admire him, he might as well do it with gusto.

For the rest of the afternoon, Austin's vocabulary was limited to oohs and wows. Exhausted from a full day of excitement, he was quiet with sleepiness on the way home. With nightfall, when they were halfway home, his head found Abby's shoulder. As he snored softly, Abby slipped an arm around his shoulder to cuddle him close and smoothed hair back from his forehead. "He's had a busy day."

Jack peered at them in the dark confines of the truck. She looked so right with a child in her arms. With the two of them, he felt a solace and happiness he hadn't known in years. She would be good for him, but he wasn't sure the opposite was true. Seeing her like this, with the boy, he knew even more than before that she would want security and the home with the white picket fence.

Abby stirred from her seat after Jack braked the truck near the back door of the lodge. Before she could gather Austin in her arms, he came around and picked him up. As if they belonged together, Austin shifted his head on Jack's shoulder and wrapped a slim arm around his neck. Never had she expected this. They'd grown so close, so quickly.

Inside Austin's room, they worked together to undress him. It was a moment Abby would treasure, remember forever. She accepted that she had to tell Jack the truth. But she couldn't get the words out. Not yet. She wanted tonight. One more night.

"I have an idea," Jack whispered close behind her.

On a sigh, she turned in his embrace. "Is it relaxing?"

"Not too." In response, she murmured something against his lips. Jack didn't know what she'd said. It didn't matter. As her arms coiled around his neck, he tasted the sweetness of her lips, then lifted her into his arms.

Before they reached her room, he was ready for her. It took effort, control. Even as he wanted to lose himself in the moment, in her, he wanted to give her time. But she fueled him as she tugged at his shirt. As she yanked at his belt buckle and shoved at his jeans, an urgency swept over him.

In the shadowy darkness of the room, he lowered her to the bed. Her dark hair fanned the white pillowcase, making her look more fragile.

· He didn't want to feel weak. He didn't want his mind muddled. But her leg wrapped around his, and she was against him. She tasted warm. Enticing. He heard her moan as she molded herself into him. Sensation, a sweet gnawing, rippled through him. With the tip of his tongue, he slowly grazed delicate skin and tasted her—touched her. Nothing seemed like enough. His mind filled with her scent, her taste, her caress. He wanted all he could have with her.

"Love me," Abby whispered. Her heart thundering, she clutched at his arms. She wanted no time to catch her breath. With desire lapping at her, she strained to bind them even closer. All the doubts, all the fears, were forgotten. Her fingers gliding over him, she wrapped her legs around his buttocks and took him into her. Through a cloud of sensation, she heard his harsh breaths as she moved at first slowly, then faster with him. Passion consumed her, controlled her. Pleasure filling her, she drifted under desire's spell. Breathless now, she closed her eyes as the wildness—the frenzy began.

Chapter Ten

Staying the night with Abby had never entered Jack's mind—not with Austin in the other room. So he'd gone back to his place and after waking up he took a morning ride, then helped Guy repair a hayride wagon. Though he'd stayed clear of any decision making about the ranch, he'd willingly helped Guy or Ray or one of the ranch hands with everyday jobs. He believed Ray could handle the ranch for now, and retire when Sam returned from his honeymoon.

At the edge of the ranch buildings, Jack dismounted and led Roper toward the stable. But if Sam had envisioned a different kind of ending, that was his problem for becoming prone to wishful thinking. In Jack's mind, all that had been wrong between them still existed.

Passing a corral that was used for foals, he saw several ranch hands gathered near. One of them raised his head, and then the others did the same. Jack knew he'd become the hot topic. A hand named Leo said something to the others, then hustled over. ''Sorry to bother you, Jack. But I—uh, we—'' He gestured at the other ranch hands. ''We think something is wrong. Ray ain't around.''

At what point would the men accept that he wasn't their boss anymore, that the comings and goings at the ranch weren't his business? ''Find Sam.''

Leo fell in step beside him. ''Ray hasn't come out of his place yet. That's not like him.'' Worry was clearly etched in the man's face. ''It's past daybreak, and I can't just barge into his place.''

Jack would have liked to believe Ray had overslept, but not once in more than three decades of working for Sam had he ever done that. Jack handed the horse's reins to another ranch hand standing nearby. ''Take him for me.''

Behind the stable area was a small cottage where Ray had lived since he'd come to the ranch over thirty years ago. On the wooden porch of the white house with its blue shutters, Jack knocked on the door. ''Have you got anyone looking for Guy?'' he asked Leo. If something was wrong or had happened to Ray, Guy, as his nephew, needed to be told.

''Andy went to get him,'' Leo said.

Jack rapped again, then tried the door. Twice he jiggled the doorknob to confirm that the door was locked. Leaving it, he walked to the kitchen window. Beneath his feet, the boards of the old porch squeaked. After a look in the window revealed nothing, he returned to the door and slammed a foot against it as a sense of urgency rushed through him. A step from the bedroom doorway, he saw Ray sprawled across the bed. ''He's here,'' Jack called out, and rushed to him.

''Don't feel so good,'' Ray muttered when Jack bent over him. ''I got up, but—'' Sweating, he looked pale. ''I know I'm late.''

''Jeez, stop worrying about that.'' Concern rippled through him for his good friend. ''Do you hurt?''

''Pain right here.'' He jabbed a tanned and brown-spotted, leathered-looking hand at his chest.

Jack already had the phone in his hand. ''Think he's having a heart attack,'' he told the 911 operator.

Within two hours, Ray was resting more peacefully after receiving a blood thinner and beta-blocker to dissolve a blood clot. Once Wendy and Guy arrived to stay with Ray, Jack left to go back to the ranch. There he found Sam, recently returned from a one-day trip to Flagstaff.

''I can't believe it.'' Disbelief cut deep lines into Sam's face as Jack told him about Ray.

''We should go to the hospital now,'' Laura said, clutching Sam's hand.

Jack noticed Abby sitting on a chair in the corner of Sam's office, cradling a sleeping Jodi. He'd wondered who was watching Wendy and Guy's daughter. "They could use some more support." Looking back at his father, he saw his hesitancy. Jack guessed why. "Go," he said. He figured he owed both men. Ray had been there when Sam had placed Jack on his first horse. Ray had taught him to lasso a calf. He'd ridden alongside Sam and Ray in a roundup. "I'll keep an eye on everything."

Abby exchanged a quick look with her aunt and felt hope rise. Despite Jack's insistence that he wanted no involvement with the ranch business, when he was needed he'd offered to help.

Abby cared for Jodi until Wendy's sister came for her. At one-thirty, after getting Austin settled in a wood-carving class, she met her aunt in the lobby for a drive to town to pick up their dresses for the wedding.

Beside her in the car, her aunt opened her purse and hunted inside it. "I left Sam at the hospital. Ray won't need a bypass operation."

"I'm glad to hear that. He's been such a sweet man to me." Abby kept her eyes on the truck ahead of them.

"Sam and I thought about postponing the wedding, but we couldn't call it off with out-of-state guests already here, staying in motels."

"I'm sure Ray didn't expect you to."

Her aunt withdrew a tissue and dabbed at perspiration above her upper lip. "Sam told me that was what Ray said the moment he walked into his room. He insisted we go ahead with the wedding." She looked as if she was trying hard to keep her spirits bright. "But tomorrow, when the wedding is over, we'll go see him, take him a slice of wedding cake."

"Was anything said about when he might come home?"

"Three or four days." Worry clouded her aunt's eyes. "Sam and I have decided not to take our honeymoon."

Abby hated to see anything lessen her aunt's happiness. "Oh, Aunt Laura, Ray would want you to."

Her aunt sent her a quick smile. "Yes, I think he would, too, but we really don't have a choice. Sam can't get away. With Ray ill, who would run the ranch?"

Jack was the obvious one. "What did Jack say?"

"He doesn't want to take over the ranch. It hurts Sam so that they don't get along well. I wish I could help."

No one could, Abby thought. Trust had been lost.

A side trip in town to a small boutique for panty hose and a long, white slip brought them back to the ranch at three forty-five. Abby and her aunt joined Sam and the others poolside for the wedding rehearsal.

As ever, Laura had recaptured her bright spirit. Happy and smiling, her aunt took her place beside Sam and listened dutifully to the minister's instructions. Afterward, with a hand on Austin's shoulder, she assured him, "You get the second piece of the wedding cake tomorrow."

The rehearsal ended, and everyone gathered in the dining room for dinner. Sitting with Jack and Austin,

Abby let herself pretend for one night that they were a family. They seemed like one as they talked and laughed and shared a taste of some tidbit from the other's plate.

While Jack and Austin were talking to an old friend of Sam's, Abby conversed with one of the lodge guests about the Boston symphony.

Next time she broke free of the woman expounding on her cruise to Mexico, Abby saw Jack at another table talking to Wendy and Guy who'd just returned from the hospital. After a few more minutes of polite listening, Abby excused herself.

Standing beside Jack, Austin had curled an arm around Jack's neck as if it was the most natural thing in the world.

Abby settled on a nearby chair. "What did Guy say about Ray? Is he all right?"

He heard anxiousness in her voice and covered her hand with his own. "Better than that. He should be home in two days. He has new medicine and an exercise program."

"I thought he had one from the last time."

"He did. This time he's going to follow it." Jack chuckled. "That's what Guy said." Beside him, he felt Austin inch closer and raised his hand from the boy's back to ruffle his hair. To have the small body so near was a new and different feeling, a good one, damn good. "Did you ever get your ice cream?"

"Uh-huh." Austin answered on a nod. "Remember when you said you'd show me how to shoe a horse? Could we do that tomorrow?"

Jack had intended to do that today, but Ray's illness had kept him preoccupied. "Can't. Tomorrow is the wedding. We'll do it the day after," he promised. Jack watched him dart a troubled look at Abby. "What's the problem?"

"We'll be leaving in the morning," Abby answered. Even saying the words wasn't easy. She watched the play of emotions, the disappointment, that had stolen Austin's smile. Leaving meant letting go of something he'd found at the ranch, something he'd never had, a man who seemed to want to be part of his life, who'd spent time teaching him, listening to him, holding him.

"When's your flight?"

"In the morning. Before eleven," Abby answered.

Jack called himself an idiot. Of course, they'd be leaving. He'd made plans to be in Cheyenne for a rodeo, hadn't he? And they'd be back in Boston. He was still getting a grip on that news when a sense of loss hit him. The warmth was suddenly gone from his side. As if he'd never been next to him, Austin had left. "I'll figure out some time to show him how to shoe a horse," Jack said.

Abby sent him a thank-you smile for understanding how important this was to the boy. Austin would have bragging rights when he returned to the city. She looked to see Austin now standing by a group of friends. Her heart went out to him. He was his mother's child. He laughed, but the joy never reached his eyes. How often had she put on a brave face when she'd had to leave a friend just made? On the day Austin was born, she'd vowed he'd have roots, stability, and years with friends to avoid too many moments like this. That was a promise she planned to keep.

Before guests began to leave, it was after ten o'clock. Running out of energy, Austin had found a chair away from everyone. Slouched on it, he repeatedly yawned.

"He's had it," Jack said. He'd already decided on a new plan. If he could rouse Austin early enough in the morning, he'd show him how to shoe the horse then.

Abby checked her wristwatch. It was later than she'd thought. "I'd better take him upstairs."

Jack released his hold on her. "I'll meet you up there."

"Okay." She needed time alone with him. Tonight, seeing the way Austin had been with Jack, forced a decision on her. She had to tell Jack the truth. After saying good-night to her blissful aunt and to several others, Abby urged Austin toward their rooms.

Before she had the door unlocked, Jack arrived with a tray from the kitchen containing what he called "real coffee." She left him sitting on one of the sofas while she helped Austin get ready for bed. Tired, nearly asleep in his clothes, he flopped back on the bed, letting her undress him.

"He's out?" Jack whispered close behind her.

"Definitely." Abby swayed as Jack snaked an

arm around the front of her waist and drew her back against him.

"You feel wonderful," he murmured into the curve of her neck.

Oh, how she wished she could stop time, freeze the moment. But there was no backing away now. She had to tell him.

The tension in her body was so slight that Jack thought he'd imagined it, then the small of her back seemed to draw inward. "Hey." He pulled back, touched her shoulders to turn her. In the shadowed room, he searched her face. "Why the frown?" he asked about the deepening line between her eyebrows.

Desperately she wanted to cling to him, beg him not to be angry. *Oh, Jack, forgive me. Please, forgive me.*

"Who are you worrying about? Your aunt's happy. Ray's going to be okay. And—oh, yeah." He smiled, hoping his news would make her smile. "Guy's leaving rodeo. So you don't have to worry about him and Wendy. Earlier, he told me that he's staying here."

"I'm glad." She meant that, but it was so hard to feel anything for anyone else at the moment.

"I thought he should have quit." As she stepped away, into the other room, her tension passed to him. There was something—something in the air. His gut knotted because she wasn't acting like herself. "But it wasn't my business to tell him that," he said absently.

With deliberation, she placed space between them. Now, Abby, she berated herself. Don't be a coward. Tell him. "It isn't easy having a child in your life when you want to rodeo. A child can slow you down."

Jack's frown deepened. Was she trying to tell him that she didn't think the life he led was right for a kid? "I've seen others travel with their families. But Wendy wanted to settle down. Guy needed to face that. He needed to think about Jodi." He waited for her gaze to meet his. Though several feet separated them, he saw the glistening of tears in her eyes. "What's wrong?"

Guilt enveloped her. He would never forgive her. He'd never understand. "What if he…?" She choked out the words. "What if Austin was yours?"

"What if…?" He wasn't sure what she was asking. Did she want to know if he loved Austin enough to sacrifice for him? More than once, he'd tried to rationalize his feelings about the boy. "The more I'm with Austin, the more I forget he's someone else's. Is that what you're really asking?"

Abby's heart tightened. "No." *Oh, God.* Tears slipped out. She couldn't stop them. "Jack, I'm sorry. I really am. I should have told you. I know I should have."

"Told me…?" He didn't need her to say more. In a heartbeat, everything in the room faded except her face. He stared hard at her, sensing the words not yet said. Maybe she was joking, or testing him. No smile on her lips. No tease in her eyes. In them, shining with tears, he saw the truth. ''Abby, he isn't—'' He couldn't finish asking her the question.

It hurt to breathe. She nodded. ''He's your son.'' He looked stunned, standing still as if frozen, so still she thought he'd stopped breathing. Then suddenly he spun away and charged toward the other room. What was he going to do? Her heart pounding with uncertainty, she reached the doorway to see him standing beside the bed, simply staring down at Austin.

Stupid, Jack mused. He'd seen Abby in the boy's face, but the smile was—Sam's, his own, he realized now. Why hadn't he let himself see that before this? Maybe because he liked the boy, because, he thought almost painfully now, he loved Abby, and it was easier to believe the boy was another man's than to imagine she'd kept them apart. So he hadn't allowed himself to see the truth.

Anger rose, settled in his throat, tightening it. Not wanting to wake Austin, he crossed back to Abby at the doorway, took her arm and propelled her to the other room. ''Why didn't you tell me?'' he asked in an angry whisper. He released her before he lost good sense. ''Why? Just tell me why, dammit. Did you know you were pregnant before you left?''

''Yes, I knew.'' Abby looked for words to defend her actions. ''Jack, think back. Remember how it was. You told me about your mother.''

He was in no mood for verbally dancing around each other. ''What does she have to do with this?''

He didn't understand, or wouldn't. "I didn't think you wanted a child—ever.''

Jack avoided her eyes. "That wasn't true anymore.''

"I didn't know that." Some of the heartbreak she'd felt years ago returned. "I was pregnant, and the man I loved had left. No goodbye. Nothing. Why would I want to find you, tell you I was pregnant? To make you stay with me? You didn't think enough of me to stay. I didn't want to trap you.''

"I told you what happened. I told you about the divorce papers. You could have told me the truth days ago.''

"Mom?''

Austin's sleepy voice made Jack turn around, and made Abby jump.

Half-asleep, Austin stood in the doorway rubbing his eyes. "Are you yelling?''

"No, sweetheart." Abby was already by him, kneeling to his level and touching his shoulders. How would he feel about the news that Jack was his father?

For the second time in as many minutes, she jumped as Jack shut the door hard behind him. Her arms around Austin, she cuddled him to her. "You should go back to sleep, honey.''

"Mom—''

"Shh." She spoke softly, aware how attuned he was to her moods. No matter what happened with Jack, she would somehow protect Austin from being hurt by either of them.

* * *

Leaving her didn't help. Jack swore under his breath while he descended the stairs. He couldn't walk away from the ache within him. The two people he'd loved the most had deceived him. He was so damn tired of the lies. Hers. His father's. People he loved. People he trusted. Damn, how could Abby have done this to them?

He entered Sam's office, intending to snag a bottle from a credenza. The office wasn't empty. Sam sat behind the enormous walnut desk. Jack said nothing and crossed to where Sam stocked the liquor. Sam had started all the lies, hadn't he? This whole mess had begun with his lie. "I guess you should know." He grabbed the bottle by the neck. "You're a grandpa."

"I'm...?" Shock crossed Sam's face. Slowly he set the pencil in his hand down on the tally sheet before him. "A grandpa?"

With effort, Jack checked his temper. If he let it go, it would take control. "Abby told me that Austin is mine."

"Yours? But—when did you learn this?" he asked with a look of incredulity.

"Minutes ago."

"Why didn't she tell you before this?"

"Good question. But you don't want to hear the answer."

Questions filled Sam's pale eyes. "You're not happy about the news?"

Did his father really expect him to sound joyful? "Eight years ago I might have been."

Sam's frown deepened. "You don't want the boy?"

God, how could he even ask that? "Of course I want him. This isn't about Austin. This is about her, about what Abby did."

Sam came around to the front edge of the desk. "I'm at a loss to understand this. But I can't believe she didn't have a good reason."

"Save it. She had no right to keep him from me."

Confusion colored Sam's voice. "Did you ask her why she did? None of this makes sense. It's clear she loves you."

"Don't!" Jack sliced a hand at the air. "I don't want to hear that."

"You don't want to hear what? The truth?"

All that had passed between them before seemed a breath away. Jack set the bottle on the desk, hard. "Everyone is suddenly so willing to tell the truth. Why not before? Why is it that the truth is so long in coming from *both* of you?" he snapped, unable to quell the fury growing within him.

Having stepped near, Sam stopped himself from reaching out.

Jack knew he'd been about to offer a comforting touch, a sympathetic pat. He didn't want either, especially from him. "Do you really want to know what her reason was?" Jack didn't wait for an answer. "She said she didn't tell me because of what I felt about a woman risking too much, risking her life to have a child.'' Sam paled. Jack didn't care. ''Remember that? Remember that's what I felt because I thought my mother died giving birth to me, because my father told me that for years? Do you remember all that, Sam?''

''That's why she didn't tell you?''

''Yeah. She knew I didn't want kids. Of course I didn't. I didn't want to be responsible for another woman's death. But then I learned that I never was, didn't I?''

''This was all my fault then?''

''Damn straight it was,'' Jack yelled. He'd thought the anger at his father had passed, but it exploded from him. ''Yes, it's your fault. How could it not be? *You* made me believe my birth was responsible for her dying. That influenced everything I did, what I felt about Abby, what I thought I could give her, have with her.''

''Jack, I'm sorry. I—I know that those words don't undo the harm, but—''

''No, they don't.'' He'd spent eight years with a bomb ticking inside him, Jack realized. ''You know what I don't understand? Why did you think that it would be easier for me to accept a lie than the truth, than knowing she left for a career in dancing, for more excitement in her life? Or wasn't that why she left? Maybe all of this was about you. Not her.''

Sam shrugged, started to turn away.

Jack had had it. ''Tell me,'' he said furiously, grabbing Sam's shoulder and turning him to face him. ''Was the lie to save your *precious* pride?''

Anger clenched his father's jaw. As a child, Jack had seen the look once, the time that two men from some development company had been trying to intimidate ranchers into selling their land. His father had led the group of ranchers, looked the same way, and gone nose-to-nose with one of the developers before making it clear that no one was selling.

"Tell me," Jack prodded, pushing Sam to his limit. In that instant, he realized he almost wished his father would get so angry he would throw a punch. "This was about your pride, wasn't it?"

Sam's jaw softened. A dullness clouded his blue eyes, a look of resignation slouched his shoulders. As if in pain, he rubbed a hand over the back of his neck. "She left me for another man, not to pursue a dancing career."

Jack had guessed as much years ago. So all the secrets were because his father had been humiliated, because he'd been rejected. If only Sam had been straight with him from the beginning, everything would be different now. He'd have told Abby how much he loved her. She'd have told him she was pregnant. They'd have shared the joy of that moment, been together. He'd have seen his son born, watched him take his first step, heard him say his first word. All that he'd lost was because of Sam.

"I never meant—" Sam gave his head a shake as if trying to banish a thought. "I didn't know I'd cause all of this with—"

"With your lie?" Jack expected no response. Too much fury filling him, he walked toward the door, needing to leave, to get away from Sam before he said more harsh words that could never be forgotten.

They'd been close, truly close, as much friends as father and son, especially after Jack had grown up. At least they had been before that fateful day when he'd found the divorce papers.

If he'd known the truth, his thoughts about his mother might have changed, but his feelings for Sam would have deepened with that knowledge. After all, his father had stayed, his father had been faithful to his marriage vows.

Jack placed a hand on the doorknob. But he never opened the door. Like a slow-moving wave, a realization began to flow over his anger, his hurt. His father had raised and loved him; she hadn't. Jack let go of the doorknob and turned around. She'd left Sam, but she'd also left him, hadn't she? There was no other explanation. If that wasn't true, he'd have been with her and not Sam.

His back to him, Sam stood by the window.

All this time, there had been one reason for Sam's lie. The need for more than words consuming him, Jack moved behind his father, touched his shoulder. "Dad."

Beneath the shadowed light in the room, when Sam faced him, Jack saw the sorrow that he'd inflicted. God, how wrong he'd been. "I'm not a kid. I don't need protecting anymore."

A pained look etched deeper lines in his father's face. "I don't know what you're talking about."

Jack forced out what he viewed as the final secret.

"She never wanted me, did she? That's what you didn't want me to know. She hadn't wanted me."

Sam heaved a sigh and straightened his back as if he were lifting a burden he'd carried too long. "I didn't want you to be hurt." For a second, he closed his eyes as if anguishing. "And look how much hurt I've caused you."

"We've hurt each other." Jack placed an arm around his father's shoulders. This man had been willing to take every angry word Jack had tossed at him, even now, just to protect him. "I'm sorry, Dad." No words could erase all the wrong ones he'd said to him. "I'm really sorry."

Chapter Eleven

Jack dealt with guilt after leaving his father. He'd always considered himself a reasonable man. What he'd been was a fool. He'd condemned Sam, had played jury and executioner, and during a few painful moments of realization with his father, all the love, the friendship, the devotion they'd shared for years had returned.

Unable to sleep, he took a ride at sunrise. As if as one with him, Roper reacted to his tenseness and pranced a bit with nervousness before obeying Jack's touch on the reins.

With the sound of bawling cattle surrounding him, he slowed the horse and leaned forward in the saddle to rub his throbbing knee. Damp morning air always reminded him of the injury. It wouldn't get better if he stayed in rodeo. A few more slams to the ground, a few more jolts against the wood of a chute by some rambunctious bull, and he'd be limping for the rest of his life.

Nearing the stables, he slowed Roper's pace. He had nothing more to prove, not really. He possessed a world champion title several years in a row. He'd challenged most of the best animals in rodeo. He'd enjoyed the fruits of his fame and title, having had plenty of money and plenty of female company.

And the one reason for staying away from the ranch had disappeared.

He dismounted, then spent time caring for Roper. When he left the stable, he saw a florist and two catering vans parked in front of the lodge. A few guests were coming in from a morning ride. Shortly, wedding guests would begin drifting in and joining ranch guests, who'd also been invited to the ceremony.

Last night, his life, his way of thinking, everything, had changed.

He was a father.

Those four words scared him more than any one-on-one with an ornery bull.

In response to the whinny of a horse in the corral, he raised his head and nearly misstepped at the sight of Austin. He'd faced snorting bulls and mean-spirited horses, drunken cowboys and irritated women, and he'd never felt his stomach somersault until now.

He searched Austin's small features. The boy's

high cheekbones were like his own. Though his eyes were Abby's, the smile was his. It amazed him that he hadn't noticed that before.

Slowly they came closer. Then, feet from each other, they stopped. As worry leaped into the boy's eyes, Jack felt his stomach clench. He wanted to hug him. He'd held him before as a concerned adult, a caring friend. He wanted to hold him now as the boy's father.

"You look mad," Austin said. "Did I do something wrong?"

"Did—" Lightly, Jack placed a hand on Austin's shoulder. "You didn't do anything wrong." He sat back on the edge of a water trough to be closer to the boy's eye level.

"Mom said—"

The hesitation in his voice alerted Jack. "What did your mom say?"

"Mom said that you're my dad."

Jack quelled an urge to touch the top of Austin's head. He could hear those words from a hundred other people, and they'd never mean the same as hearing Austin say them. "Guess you want to talk."

"I—" Staring down, Austin kicked at the dirt with the toe of his shoe. Clearly he was struggling with a weighty thought.

Jack would do whatever he could to make this easier on him. "Go ahead. You can say anything."

"Are you glad?" Head still bent, Austin spoke so quietly Jack had to strain to hear him.

He never expected such a heavy-duty question,

but during the past two weeks, he'd noticed that the boy barreled without hesitation toward challenges. "Is that all you want to know?"

Head still bent, he raised his eyes to Jack. "Why didn't you come before?"

There were no easy answers. "Come with me. We need to talk." With a light touch on the boy's shoulder, Jack urged him toward the porch steps. "Let's sit up there."

"I can't get dirty." His eyebrows veed. "Mom would be really mad."

"I have an idea." Jack went up to the porch and yanked a cushion from one of the chairs, then dropped it onto the step. "Here. Sit down now." As they settled beside each other, Jack remembered other times with him, sitting on a step, staring at a star-filled sky. They'd become friends then. "About what you said." *Don't put your foot in your mouth.* He didn't want to do anything that might change the way the boy was beginning to feel about him. "I didn't come because I didn't know about you. I didn't know I had a son."

"Mom didn't tell you?"

The last thing Jack wanted to do was blame Abby. "I haven't seen your mom in a long time."

Austin nodded slowly as if confirming his words. "That's what she said."

Jack couldn't lie, pretend Abby hadn't known where he was. The boy was too sharp to accept that. "Austin, your mom didn't know how much I would want you."

The deep brown eyes locked with his. "Yeah?"

"Yeah," Jack assured him. "How do you feel about having me for your dad?"

In a deciphering manner, for the longest damn moment of Jack's life, Austin studied him closely. "I like the idea," he finally said. "I'm glad."

Jack's chest filled with emotion. "You are?"

"Uh-huh." Shifting, Austin sat with his knees touching Jack's leg. "I liked you a lot even before I knew you were my dad."

Was there a better compliment from one's child? A sense of relief flowed through him. How often had the sight of Austin's smile roused him from a foul mood? How often had the boy's childish laughter made him forget how many problems existed in his life? And then had come the real clincher, hadn't it? When Austin had hugged him, he'd wished for a son like him. No, he'd wished Austin had been his.

"What about you?" A frown appeared on the boy's young face. "Are you really glad?"

"Austin." Jack put his arm around the boy's shoulders. "There isn't anyone I'd rather have for my son. Yes, I'm glad," he said, using the boy's words. "I'm really glad." He's mine, Jack mused as Austin flung his arms around Jack's midsection. He ran a gentle hand over the boy's head. He couldn't recapture the years lost, but he could give Austin a father for all the tomorrows to come.

"I'll tell you a secret," Jack said as he drew back to look down at him. "We need to find Sam." He spoke conspiratorially. "He's nervous about getting married. If we were with him, that would help him a lot." Unwilling to let go yet, he kept the boy's small hand in his and pushed to his feet. "You know he's your grandpa."

Austin's eyes went wide. "He is?"

"That's right."

"Wow! I got a grandpa, too?"

"You got one of them, too." And this ranch, he mused. But there was plenty of time to explain all that to him. Plenty of time.

Abby finished dressing now that Austin had left. She prayed that he stayed clean before the wedding, but she'd decided to get him together first, then herself. She needed time alone.

Sitting on the chair, she closed her eyes for a moment as she remembered the look that had flashed across Austin's face when she told him about Jack. Pure joy. He'd been so good, so incredible. It hadn't really mattered to him why he hadn't had Jack before. All that he'd cared about was that he had a father now. And that father was someone he really wanted in his life.

You're lucky, Abby. He could have cried or shown a flare of temper, been angry the way his father was. Or he could have drilled her with more questions about why she hadn't told him sooner.

Wandering to the window, she wondered where he'd gone. It didn't take long for her to get an answer to her question.

She saw them, her son and the man she loved, walking, hands clasped. Her son's face angled up toward his father's, and they were both smiling. Abby gave thanks that they'd found each other.

But breathing suddenly hurt. She'd always thought of herself as an honest woman, until now. An omission of truth was as good as a lie. And achingly she wished for a replay button, a way to transcend time for one second, to be able to say to him eight years ago, "I'm having your baby."

She squeezed her eyes tight and fought the threat of tears. Sadness, uncertainty, even relief that he finally knew the truth wove together within her. Tears wouldn't change anything, she reminded herself while crossing to the closet for the blue dress with its lacy bodice.

Whatever they, as a family, could have had slipped from her grasp on the day she'd decided to keep her secret. Zipping up the dress, she knew now that she'd made a mistake. But it was too late to change anything.

After a quick glance in the mirror, she headed for the door. If no one looked too closely, they wouldn't see the circles under her eyes from a lack of sleep last night. She wanted nothing to spoil this day for her aunt. Stepping out of the room, she geared herself mentally for seeing Jack. They had to be amiable.

Instead of heading for her aunt's room, she went to the kitchen, hoping that time with Wendy would lighten her mood. Though dressed for attending the wedding, Wendy wore an apron that covered her pale pink dress from her chest to her knees.

All nervous energy this morning, her friend scurried around the kitchen, handling small details. "Count the silverware," she instructed one worker. "That way we'll know if any accidentally makes its way to the garbage can." Spotting Abby, she waved a fork at her. "You look like a bride yourself."

Abby returned the expected smile. "Thanks." Behind Wendy, the caterer was barking instructions. "Why are you working? Aren't you a guest today?"

Her friend shrugged a shoulder. "Yes, I am, but it's hard to relinquish my kitchen to anyone," she admitted while reaching back to untie her apron.

Abby crossed to the refrigerator. "I came for the bouquets."

"I had to protect them," Wendy whispered to Abby, and peered with her into the opened refrigerator. "That tall guy with the catering company almost smashed them with the tray of cheese puffs."

Abby removed the bouquets and Austin's boutonniere. Similar to her bouquet with its gardenia, lilies, baby's breath and carnations, the bride's also contained white tea roses. "They look lovely, don't they?"

"I've always liked gardenias."

"There you are." Guy stood in the doorway, little Jodi in his arm. In a paler pink dress than her mother's, Jodi looked adorable, as picture perfect with her soft brown curls and dimpled smile as a child model. "Out of the kitchen." Guy moved near his wife, then swept his free arm toward the door.

The humorous moment helped. "I told her the same thing," Abby said.

"All right. All right." Wendy raised her hands in surrender.

Abby left them and rushed up the steps to her aunt's room.

Standing before the mirror, Laura looked so pretty. She'd chosen a long-sleeve, tea-length, champagne-colored slip dress with lace overlay.

"I'm feeling giddy," she admitted on a girlish laugh.

"You're supposed to be." Positioned behind her, Abby fussed over the thin wreath of blue forget-me-nots and sprigs of baby's breath in Laura's hair. "Now you have something blue. Do you have something old?"

Laura swiveled on the stool and took Abby's hands. "Something is wrong, isn't it?"

Abby fiddled with the long, champagne-colored ribbons trailing from her aunt's bouquet. She thought she'd hidden her sadness. But Laura had always been able to read her moods well. "They both know. Jack and Austin."

An anxious frown wiped away the glow on the older woman's face. "You told them."

"Yes." *And my world fell apart.*

Laura tightened her grip. "Abby, that's best. It really is."

Though Abby hadn't thought so during that moment of revelation, she knew her aunt was right. It would have been wrong and unfair to keep Austin and Jack apart.

"Was Jack terribly angry?"

Desperately she'd been trying to forget how cold and distant he'd looked before leaving her. "Terribly."

Laura pulled her into her arms. "If he loves you, his anger won't last."

Abby doubted that wishful thinking would work. Love didn't always conquer all. "Now, do you have something borrowed?" she asked, to end the melancholy mood on what should have been the happiest day of her aunt's life.

Laura pointed with a fingertip at her ear. "That would be your pearl earrings."

Abby touched Laura's shoulders, then leaned forward and kissed her cheek. "So, you're all set."

"And so—so nervous." Laura inhaled deeply. "Abby, I feel as if I'm a teenager. I swear, if I start giggling in the middle of the ceremony—"

"You won't."

"I could. Nervousness and giggles are a family trait. Uncle Gregory's wife giggled at his funeral."

Abby had never met Uncle Gregory or his wife. In fact, until she was nineteen, she'd seen her aunt only a few times during the years she was growing up. She and her mother had constantly moved. Only after her mother's death had she and Laura gotten so close.

"Oh, Abby." Her happiness overwhelming her,

Laura caught her hand again. "I'm so happy. Sam is so wonderful."

She's glowing, Abby mused. "Yes, he is."

"I know you were concerned about me moving here, but I don't need five-star restaurants, and the theater and art galleries to be happy. I need Sam."

She'd felt the same way about Jack, never doubting she'd find happiness at the ranch as long as she was with him.

While Laura made a last-minute stop in the washroom, Abby wandered downstairs. She'd barely stepped outside when Austin skidded to a stop in front of her.

"Come on." His smaller hand caught hers. "Wait until you see how they decorated the car."

Abby let him tug her along. "Sam's car?"

"He's my grandpa." He turned wide eyes up at her. "Did you know that?"

"Yes, I know." She hadn't mentioned Sam to him, believing that learning he had a father was enough to absorb. Abby assumed he'd talked to Jack and he'd told Austin about Sam being his grandpa.

"Isn't it neat, Mom?"

Abby viewed the car. Laughter rippled from her. She couldn't imagine Sam and her aunt going anywhere in that car. Multicolored balloons tied to the car's antenna bobbed in the air. Someone had printed the words Just Married across the back window, and just below it, Lovebirds on Board. Several sets of mismatched cowboy boots and a collection of cowbells were tied to the rear bumper. "Nothing like being inconspicuous."

Austin turned a puzzled look up at her. "Huh?"

"Never mind, honey."

"Isn't it neat?" he repeated, definitely impressed.

"Yes, it's neat." Abby bent over to pin on his boutonniere.

"Mom, I gotta go and help Guy." Impatiently he danced a two-step in place.

She made quick work of the job. "All done." She stood back, then watched him dash off to help tie on more balloons.

Fighting her own low spirits, she spent time double-checking everything, including how many folding chairs the catering-company workers had set up in each row near the pool. Sunlight glimmered off the water, a warm breeze lightly flapped at the canvas of the white tents located for dining beyond the pool area.

Abby looked over the flower arrangements, eyed the tables set with white linen and crystal and took time to admire the multitiered wedding cake that Wendy had made.

As guests arrived and were seated, she slipped into the lodge to join her nervous aunt. "It's time," Abby told her.

Standing just inside the door, Laura blew out a long breath. "I'm ready."

"And beautiful," Abby said. She gave her a quick hug before opening the terrace doors. The whinnying of horses accompanied the sound of music as Abby left the house.

Ahead of Laura, she moved past the rows of seated guests. With each step, she felt Jack's eyes on her, but she avoided meeting them. Close by his side, Austin was holding the pillow with the rings. Regret drained her. She'd spent the night and this morning wishing she'd done everything different, wishing she could go back to the magical moments eight years ago—a day ago.

Despite such thoughts, she made certain her smile never wavered. A nervous-looking Sam, standing beneath the arched trellis decorated with white tea roses, grinned back at her.

Abby took her place, then in response to the playing of the wedding processional, she turned, along with everyone else, to watch the bride.

Looking radiant, her aunt glided toward Sam. Abby dealt with the tears smarting her eyes as the minister began the wedding ceremony. At the appropriate moment, Jack's hand curled over Austin's shoulder as a signal right before he was to step forward with the rings.

The ceremony was short, but heartwarming, and as Laura and Sam finished saying their vows, then kissed, the crowd clapped and cheered. The photographer clicked away while his partner handled a video camera. The sun shone brighter.

Stepping forward, Abby fiercely hugged her aunt. "I'm so happy for you." To let other well-wishers offer congratulations, she turned away. Briefly she stood face-to-face with Jack, but didn't allow herself more than a second of eye contact. This was one of the most important days of her aunt's life. No matter how angry he was, she couldn't let him vent his wrath today and ruin these moments.

She passed time talking to several guests and sampling appetizers. While some people headed for the food table, others drew closer to the country band. Abby accompanied Austin down the buffet line and settled him at a table. When, as best man, Jack led everyone in a toast, glasses clinked along with a chorus of good wishes.

"The bride looks beautiful," a woman behind her gushed.

The last time Abby had heard those words, she'd been at Cody Slater's wedding. A rodeo buddy of Jack's, he and his bride had gotten married on their horses and served Tex-Mex food at the reception. Along with Jack, Abby had wrapped pink crepe paper around the horse saddles of the bride and groom and had attached balloons to the bridles.

It had been an unusual but fun wedding, and she and Jack had laughed while munching on tacos and burritos and barbecue ribs. Beneath the stars, they'd danced in a meadow of flowers along with other guests. Then they'd made love in the hayloft after the guests left. Everything had seemed so simple then. Everything in the world had seemed perfect.

"The wedding was perfect, wasn't it?"

Abby smiled that the words coming from one of Sam's neighbors echoed her thoughts. "Yes, it was.'' In search of Austin, she turned around. Instead, she saw Jack weaving his way toward her.

Her heart hammering in her chest, she willed herself to meet his eyes. She'd been preparing for accusations, for more anger and resentment.

''Come on,'' he said so softly she barely heard him.

As he slipped a hand beneath her elbow, Abby let him steer her away from the crowd. That he was talking to her amazed her. Clearly he planned to be civil. For that, she was grateful.

In silence, she moved with him, waiting until they stopped near the back of the lodge. Shoulders back, dread heavy in her, she raised her face to him. Because there was nothing else she could do, she spoke what was in her heart. ''I know I should have never kept Austin away from you. But you were gone.'' All she could do was explain the feelings she'd had nearly a decade ago. ''I thought you didn't love me. I really believed that you didn't want any child, that you didn't want me.''

So much had happened to Jack since he'd last talked to her. So much made more sense to him. ''I know I led you to believe that,'' he said. Because of him, her life had been more difficult. ''I'm sorry, Abby.'' He seemed to be saying that often lately. ''A lot of what went wrong was my fault.''

Nothing he said could have shocked her more. She'd expected anger. ''Oh, Jack.'' She closed her eyes as his arms wrapped around her. Relief slipping over her, she struggled against an urge to cry, and clung, knowing she loved him just as much now as she had eight years ago. "I thought—I didn't think you'd forgive me."

He wished for the years he hadn't had with Austin, would always regret missing them. But during moments of reasoning, he realized she couldn't know that all he'd said to her about no children had changed. Time with Sam last night made him aware how much a parent might do to keep their child from feeling unwanted.

With his quietness, Abby drew back to look up at him. "You talked to Austin?"

Eyes, dark and shadowed with troubled thoughts, stared up at him. "I didn't think he would know so soon."

"I never meant to keep him from you. Austin needs a father—" She paused, measured her words. "But I want him to know that you'll be near for him."

He couldn't fault her for wanting to protect their son from a father who didn't seem willing to commit to anyone. And it pained him to ask the next question. "You don't trust me, do you?" He didn't wait for an answer. He saw the truth in her eyes. He wanted to pull her close, hold her until she believed him. "I wouldn't hurt Austin. I won't. I promise." He thought about the emptiness he'd felt without her. What he wanted was here, right in front of him. "Abby, we could be a family."

Her heart stopped at the words she'd only dreamed of hearing him say. *A family.*

"I love you," he said. "I've always loved you. I want to marry you." She said nothing, did nothing. She kept staring at him with such sadness that all he longed to do was hold her, comfort, and he didn't even know why. "Say something." He realized that he'd never expected this reaction from her. "You love me, don't you?"

Heart aching, she pulled her hand free of his. "I love you. You know I do." Denying what she felt had never entered her mind. "But this isn't about me." Eight years ago, she would have flown into his arms, laughing. Eight years ago, she'd only had to think about a young girl's fantasy of marriage and children with the man of her dreams. Eight years ago, she wasn't a mother. She had a responsibility now to another person. He came first—always. "We have more to consider." How odd, she thought. She'd expected his anger, not a declaration of love when she saw him today. If only he'd said those words to her eight years ago. She'd have said yes then without hesitation. "I can't be with you, Jack," she said softly.

Chapter Twelve

Call it arrogance, but Jack had thought by now that she would be in his arms, that she'd have agreed to spend the rest of her life with him. "Can't?"

"This isn't about you and me anymore," she tried to explain. "Loving each other isn't enough."

"Do you think I don't understand your concern for Austin?"

Abby averted her eyes to avoid seeing the questions—the hurt—in his. Behind her, she heard oohs and aahs. She looked over her shoulder to see Sam removing the blue garter from her aunt's slim leg. Soon they would cut the cake. "We need to go back."

Despite her words, she didn't move. Neither did Jack. He wondered if either of them would have if Wendy hadn't come near.

Oblivious to the tension in the air, she laughingly hooked her arm in Abby's. "Come on. Laura is going to throw the bouquet."

Jack watched Wendy pull her along and away from him. Had she refused him just to make him suffer because he'd left her eight years ago? Was she getting even? Mentally he shook his head. That wasn't Abby's way. She had an open and generous heart. The last thing she'd do was hurt someone else deliberately, even someone who deserved it, like him.

From a distance, he watched Laura throw the bouquet into the arms of the local librarian, a thirty-something woman who was being courted by the town's sheriff. Together the bridal couple cut the cake, then fed a taste of it to each other.

Nothing made sense suddenly. He loved Abby. She loved him. So how could she walk away? Softly he cursed himself. Had she wondered that same question on that night he'd left her?

Damn, he'd hurt her. Until that moment, until she'd turned away from him, he hadn't realized how much he'd hurt her. A pressure filled his chest as if a band was tightening, squeezing it. *God, Abby, I'm sorry.*

Music played, guests danced. For Abby, the celebration stretched like an eternity. She wished she could curl up somewhere. Warmth behind her eyes warned her of tears. Of course she wanted to marry him.

Of course she couldn't.

As guests began to leave, she felt free to go to her room. Austin balked about ending the day, even though it was past his bedtime, but Abby reminded him they were returning home tomorrow.

"I wish we could stay," he whined.

So did she. But wishing for something wasn't enough. She'd made a decision, the best one, she believed, for Austin's sake.

Heavy pewter clouds covered the sky the next morning, matching her spirits. She and Jack couldn't have a second chance no matter how much they loved each other. She truly believed that love wasn't enough anymore.

Aware that Sam and her aunt were leaving for the airport at eight-thirty, she dressed in a rush, then hurried downstairs.

On the lodge steps, guests and employees waited with packages of birdseed to throw at the bride and groom.

"I think this is so romantic," a female guest said to another. "We never expected to be a part of so much romance when we came here for our vacation."

"The wedding was beautiful," the other woman said.

Abby's attention shifted from them to her aunt and Sam standing on the steps. She saw Jack, in the doorway behind them. Alongside him stood their son.

"I had a wonderful night," Laura whispered in her ear.

Abby couldn't help laughing. When she drew back, she saw pure delight in her aunt's eyes. Despite her personal sadness, Abby felt such joy for the couple. When she'd come to the ranch, she'd had misgivings. But the love, so obvious between them, had taken away her doubts long ago.

"I've promised Sam that I'll do a hula for him when we get to Hawaii," Laura said, then giggled softly before stepping back.

Having overheard, Sam slipped an arm around Laura's waist and urged her down the steps. "I'm counting on it."

"Have fun," Abby called to them.

Her face bright with glee, Laura gave another wave. "We will."

Before they reached the bottom of the steps, guests lining the stairs and the way to the car showered them with birdseed.

"They look so happy," a guest beside her said.

"Yes, they do." Abby noticed that Jack had carried the luggage to the car and now stood near Sam. Body language said it all. They were closer, their shoulders touching, Sam's head inclined toward Jack's as they laughed about something Sam had said. There had been a change between them since yesterday. Before her were the loving father and son she'd met years ago.

Abby watched Laura and Sam drive away until dust obscured their car. With only an hour before she and Austin had to leave for the airport, she needed to remind Austin to stay close to the lodge.

He looked sad at having to say goodbye. She would need to remind him that when he came back to the ranch, one of his new friends might be vacationing here again. Because, of course, he'd come back. This was where his grandpa and their aunt lived. This was his father's home.

Clutching the birdseed netting, she pivoted to reenter the lodge and found herself face-to-face with Jack.

"We're going to talk." Whatever was wrong between them, he planned to fix it. During a night that had stretched so long he'd nearly left his bed to dress and go to her room, he'd thought of a dozen questions. But pounding on her door at three in the morning bordered on stupidity. After everything he'd done to her in the past, he didn't need to make her the focal point of gossip, too.

Then this morning something clicked in his brain. She'd said loving each other wasn't enough. And it finally hit him what she meant.

Abby curled her fingers over the banister. All morning she'd tried to prepare for the moment when she'd face Jack again. "Jack, nothing has changed since last night."

"You're wrong. A lot has changed. I know that I was an idiot yesterday. I said marry me and offered you nothing. I know you need a home, security." He'd expected a smile then, some hint of joy, but he saw no light in her eyes. Even as he felt nerves tightening within him, he went on, ''What if I said I wasn't going back to rodeo? What if I planned to stay at the ranch?''

Abby heard him and still didn't believe what he'd said. There wasn't anything he could have said to her that would have whipped as much confusion through her. ''Why are you doing this?''

''I'm doing it because I want to, because I want to be here. Sam and I worked out our problem.''

Aware of how much hurt had existed between father and son, she felt only joy for him.

''And if I don't get out, retire, some ornery bull might get the best of me.''

She didn't need a picture drawn. She'd seen other men beaten by rodeo, their bodies broken, their spirits battered. She knew some had died in the arena, not only inexperienced ones, but also men driven past their prime, addicted to the thrill.

Jack touched her chin, forced her eyes to meet his. Such sadness shadowed them. ''Hey?''

''I'm glad you're quitting.''

''It's time.'' Lightly Jack touched her waist. ''And it's time for us. I want you and Austin to stay with me here.''

She didn't doubt he believed what he was saying. But how long would he feel that way? ''What about the championship? Aren't you going to compete for it this year?''

She wasn't listening. No, that wasn't true. She was listening, but she wasn't believing, Jack realized. ''It's just another belt buckle now.''

That wasn't true. She knew it was more. Endorsements. Commercials. Was he really willing to give up all the fame and money?

"You don't believe me?"

She longed to. "I want to."

Trust. He drew a deep breath. This was all about trust. "If you love me—" He stopped as she shook her head.

Abby swallowed against the emotion closing her throat. He was making everything harder. Her throat felt dry. He didn't understand. "What if I change my life for you, and you decide later that you made a mistake? What if we give up everything we have in Boston, and a few weeks or a month from now, you decide you miss rodeo?"

A mixture of exasperation and frustration whipped through him. Was everything slipping from his grasp because of what ifs? "Abby, that's not going to happen."

Desperately she wanted to believe him, but couldn't. "I can't risk letting Austin get hurt."

Apparently the promise he'd made last night to her didn't matter. "I told you—promised—" He stifled the urge to yell at her. "I promised that I wouldn't hurt him." How could he get her to believe him? "Trust sometimes comes on faith alone, Abby. I learned that the hard way. If I'd had more faith in Sam, I'd have realized sooner that whatever he'd done he'd been doing it for me." He wanted to hold her tight until she believed him, but she pulled back. "What are you afraid of?"

"I'm not afraid. This isn't about me. It's about Austin. It's about protecting him."

He reached out, but his hand never touched her. As quickly as he'd begun the motion, he stopped it, jamming his hand into his jeans pocket. "I'm not giving up. This isn't the end." Eyes, dark and wet, met his. "I want forever, Abby."

All that she longed for stood before her. But she carried a fear that he couldn't suppress with a few promises. "All I ask is that you be there when he needs you. Don't hurt him. Don't let him down."

For the second time in twenty-four hours, Jack watched her walk away from him.

Abby hadn't expected time or distance to make the separation from Jack easier for Austin. Before they left the ranch, she'd felt her heart twist as Austin had flung his arms around Jack's neck. For a long moment, as if it was too painful to move away, they'd stood together.

Head down, Austin had left Jack's arms and rushed to her. He'd avoided her stare when he climbed into the rental car, but Abby had seen the tears glistening in his eyes. Nothing would be easy for him anymore. His love was being pulled in two directions. While he would want to be with her in Boston, he knew a different world now with Jack.

They returned home on Sunday. By Friday, she still wasn't in step with the city's quicker tempo. She rushed from the bus and walked at a clipped pace toward home, and was half an hour late picking

Austin up from the baby-sitter's. Though pizza muffins, a favorite of Austin's, sounded like less than healthy fare, she chose that for dinner because he never balked at eating a salad with them. While she assembled everything, Austin used the time before dinner to take a bath.

Despite all the turmoil in her life, there was something comforting about being home, about being surrounded by familiar things. She'd worked hard to make a home for her and Austin. She'd saved for weeks to buy the blue paisley sofa. Some of the other furnishings, like a scarred maple breakfront, she'd found at thrift shops.

The rooms were decorated with a mixture of Early American furniture and whatever pleased her. She'd have liked a home with a yard for Austin. She'd have liked that cottage with the white picket fence. Actually, she'd have preferred a renovated barn, she thought wryly, but that was part of a fantasy. This apartment suited her, and had been home for her and Austin for the past three years.

At the sound of splashing, she wandered to the bathroom and peeked in. Her son was aiming his squirt gun at his toy boat. "Dinner is almost ready."

"Okay," he murmured. A wet washcloth was draped over his head now.

Abby stepped back before he rose from the water because he'd found modesty recently. Though they'd already fallen back into a routine, she knew he was still missing the ranch, and Jack.

She was, too, she admitted to herself as she returned to the kitchen and checked on the muffins. Even here, he was a part of them.

The moment Austin got home, he'd hung the cowboy hat from Sam on a hook that used to hold his Boston Red Sox baseball cap. He'd propped a Polaroid photo that Laura had taken of Jack and him against his Captain Cosmo bank.

More importantly, since they'd arrived home, Jack had called every night. That was good and bad. While the phone calls saved Austin from being lonely for his father, she worried about what would happen when the restless streak surfaced, and Jack was back in rodeo. A late event, a celebration, a different time zone might mean no phone call.

"Are you going to answer the phone, Mom?"

"The—" She gave her head a shake, then snatched up the receiver.

At the table, Austin ended his fascination with rolling a cherry tomato on his plate. "Who is it? Is it Dad?"

Dad. How easily he said the word. When had he begun to think of Jack that way? She nodded but held up a finger to indicate she needed time to talk to him. Friends, divorced and raising children, complained about ex-husbands and ex-wives. They either never involved themselves in their child's life, or they kept insisting on petty requests that played havoc with the child's life and emotions. Though Jack had made no demands, Abby kept expecting them. With the portable phone, she wandered to the living room so Austin wouldn't hear. "Do you plan to call next week?"

"Say hello, Abby."

"Hello."

"Better."

She heard the smile in his voice. "Jack, we need to set up a schedule so I have Austin home for your calls."

"Is this a good time?"

The lightness in his voice annoyed her. This was serious business. "Yes, this time next week would be fine."

"This time tomorrow."

She needed to make him understand why his nightly calls could cause trouble. "Jack, he'll expect you to call every night if you keep doing it."

"Then I'd better keep doing it. Tell me. Have you heard from the honeymooners?"

Abby knew that tone. He wasn't willing to listen to what made perfectly good sense to her. At least not tonight. If he was in no mood to discuss something, he could be maddeningly stubborn. "A postcard." Cradling the phone between her jaw and shoulder, now that her conversation with him wasn't something Austin couldn't hear, she returned to the kitchen to pour a cup of coffee. "My aunt wrote about leis, hula dancers and luaus."

"All Sam wrote was *Wow.*"

The humor of the situation reaching her, she laughed with him. "How wonderful."

"Mom?"

''Your son's growing impatient.''

''Can't have that. Bye, Abby.''

It was his abruptness that had her stammering. ''Uh, bye.'' She'd been dismissed, she reflected while handing the telephone receiver to Austin.

Excitement popped into the boy's voice with his greeting. ''Dad, hi!''

Frowning, Abby left the room. She'd have to make Jack listen to her. A week, a month, a year from now, would he still be calling his son? Would he still bring the same kind of joy to Austin's face? Would he be there when Austin needed him?

A week went by, school started, and she and Austin fell into a world of routines and schedules. After school, he went to the neighbor's, Mrs. Averson's. Usually Abby was home by five o'clock. Today nothing was going right.

A co-worker had knocked over her iced tea during lunch. Most of it had landed in Abby's lap, leaving a stain on her cream-colored slacks. She had to work late, missed a bus, and by the time she was a block from the bus stop, a muscle in her calf ached from a too-strenuous workout that morning in her aerobics class.

Needing to stop, she detoured to a Chinese take-out across the street and picked up sweet-and-sour pork for dinner. Thoughts of a long bath accompanied her walk home. A step in the door, she kicked off her shoes, grabbed a can of soda and was heading for the sofa when the doorbell rang. She'd thought she'd have some quiet time before Austin came home from his Cub Scout meeting.

Keeping the chain in place, she opened the door and peeked out. A florist deliveryman grinned at her. For a long moment after she accepted the glossy white box, she simply stared at it. This wasn't fair. Not fair at all. As she lifted the lid and pushed back the green tissue, her heart thundered. Why? Why was he making this so difficult?

Her hand shook as she read the card.

Love you,
Jack

Clutching it, she raised one of the long-stemmed red roses from its bed of white baby's breath and green ferns.

"I'm home, Mom."

The rose in her hand, Abby spun around.

He was scowling at her. "You didn't have the door locked," he said in a chiding tone that made her smile.

She had forgotten one of the house rules in her shock at getting the flowers.

"What's that?" he asked about the box in her hand.

His gaze lowered, making her look down, making her aware she was absently fingering the petal of a flower. "Roses."

Curious, he stepped closer and peered into the box. "Who did ya get them from?"

Abby slipped Jack's card into her pants pocket. "Your dad." As he looked up at her with wide eyes, she ran a quick finger down his nose. "Hang up your jacket now. I brought Chinese takeout home. Do you have much homework?"

"Reading." He gathered up his backpack from the chair he'd dropped it on.

"You can do that after dinner." Alone in the kitchen, she couldn't resist and inhaled the sweet fragrance of the flowers. All through dinner, her mind played tricks with her. She thought about the roses, she could even smell them, though they were in a vase in the other room. As lovely as they were, it was what they represented that was weakening her. He was romancing her, making her feel young, tempting her with fantasies. And she had to stop him before she began to believe in one special one again.

She cleaned up the kitchen after dinner and waited until Austin was busy with homework before she made a phone call. "I want to thank you," she said after his greeting. "The flowers are beautiful, but—"

Jack laughed in the soft caressing way that had always melted her. "No buts. I'm glad you like them."

If there was just the two of them, everything would be different, but she had someone else to think about. Why didn't he understand that? "Don't send any more," she insisted, determined to be firm.

"Sorry, Abby. Learn to enjoy them."

"Why?" Weakening, she felt a twinge of desperation streaking through her that he was making the situation so difficult. "Why are you doing this?" she demanded.

"Because you're wrong. Because we belong together. Because I'm not going to let you forget me."

Did he really think that was possible? He was the father of her son. He was the man she loved.

"Dad knows you like flowers, huh?" Austin mumbled between gnawing at a chicken leg after an enormous bouquet of daisies, carnations, baby's breath and daffodils arrived one evening. It was one of many flower bouquets she'd received during the past weeks. Little reminders, she assumed, recalling Jack's words.

Frowning, she took a vase from a kitchen cupboard and finished filling it with water before facing him. She didn't want Austin to get the wrong idea. "Yes, he does, but the flowers don't mean anything, Austin."

As if she'd said, "Tomorrow is Christmas," he beamed at her. "You like them, don't you?" he asked.

In an avoidance move, Abby fussed at arranging the flowers before joining him at the table. "Yes, I do."

His grin widened. "That's what he told me."

They were conspiring, she decided. "Did he?"

"Uh-huh. He said he loved you." Mouth full, he slanted a look at her.

Abby felt as if her son was viewing her through a microscope.

Dead serious, he reminded her, "That's probably why he sent them."

Who was the parent here? she wondered, not unable to see the humor in the situation.

"Dad said he'd send me chaps and spurs for my Halloween costume. You know, like the kind Guy always wears. Everyone at school knows my dad is a *real* cowboy."

"I thought—" She never finished her sentence.

"Phone's ringing, Mom." He jumped from the kitchen chair, banging it into the microwave stand behind him. "Bet that's Dad."

Abby eyed the kitchen clock above the sink. "No, it's too early." She let him answer the phone, knew by his conversation he was talking to her aunt, and then Sam. Abby stood near until he handed her the receiver. Briefly she talked with Laura about Ray.

"He's doing well. With Jack staying, Ray could retire, but Jack asked him to help until he gets back in the swing of everything."

"That's good." Had he done that to keep Ray feeling useful or was it to keep the door open? If Ray stayed on the job, Jack could leave whenever he wanted.

"Will you come for Thanksgiving?" Laura asked.

Abby hated to disappoint her, but during the past weeks, she'd been working on a series for the newspaper about the city's homeless, so leaving Boston and flying to Arizona for Thanksgiving didn't seem like a possibility. "It's doubtful," she said, and explained why.

"I wish you were coming here," Laura said.

"We'll be there for Christmas," Abby promised. Though the idea of returning to the ranch so soon was something she didn't want to do, she felt Austin needed the family gathering with Sam and her aunt, and with Jack.

"He never went back to rodeo, Abby," Laura said out of the blue. "Sam said Jack told you he wasn't planning to."

That wasn't what she'd heard. Days ago, Austin had told her that Jack planned to be in Oklahoma on Halloween night. She assumed his restless streak had returned. "He told Austin he'd be taking a trip to Tulsa for the rodeo there."

"Oh, that," her aunt said airily. "It's a public appearance for a charity rodeo. He's not on the rodeo circuit again." She was so quiet for a long moment that Abby almost squirmed. "You don't believe him, do you?"

"Aunt Laura, I think he meant what he said to me," she said honestly. "But that doesn't mean he'll stay at the ranch forever."

"No one can offer guarantees about anything."

Abby could think of other things she'd rather discuss with her aunt. "I'll try again to see if we can come for Thanksgiving."

She heard Laura sigh. "We'd really like you to come," she responded, seeming to accept Abby's desire that they change subjects. "We've missed you. So has Jack. He talks all the time about not being able to see Austin," she said, taking a three-sixty with their conversation. "After all, Abby, Austin has two homes now," her aunt reminded her.

Abby's heart stopped. Custody? Would Jack go to court, make demands? Some couples split their child's time—six months here, six months there. She couldn't stand six months away from Austin. She'd never endure even two weeks.

Perhaps he'd meant what he'd said about settling down. Then again, what if he grew restless, wanted to join the rodeo circuit again? Wasn't that her real concern? She hated her doubts about him. Oh, she hated all of this. She wanted a guarantee that he wouldn't hurt Austin. And he couldn't give her a guarantee. He couldn't prove he meant what he said, and for Austin's sake, she couldn't take any chances.

"Abby, we really have missed both of you."

"We've missed you, too." She wished she could reach through the phone and give Laura a hug.

Suddenly emerging from his bedroom, Austin stepped close. "Can I talk to Dad now?" he whispered.

"I'll ask if he's around." Abby finished talking to her aunt then asked about Jack.

"Yes, he's here. I'll get him for you."

"For Austin," Abby piped in, but she was holding a silent phone. "Here." She held it out to her son. "Aunt Laura is getting him for you."

"I'm going to a party after trick-or-treating," Austin announced the moment Jack took the phone.

Jack had come in from the corral, to see Laura on the telephone. Abby, Laura had mouthed. He'd washed his hands, grabbed a glass of ice water and was talking quietly with Sam about buying several more head of cattle when Laura had handed him the phone.

"Mom got me a black eye mask. She said there was a cowboy on TV long, long ago who wore one."

"The Lone Ranger," Jack said.

"That's him. I wanted it because my friend Carlos is wearing one and a cape."

"Who is he going to be?"

"Zorro. And know what?"

Jack loved the enthusiasm that never failed to enter Austin's voice. "What?"

"'Cause I'm going trick-or-treating when it's dark, Mom got a Princess Zelia costume, and she'll wear it when she goes with me."

Jack wished he could see that. He'd been doing a lot of wishing lately.

"Mom and me can't come for Thanksgiving,"

His son's news didn't please him. This would have been their first holiday together.

"We're going to Uncle David's house," Austin went on.

"Uncle David?" Jack didn't like the sound of this, not one bit. "Austin, is your mom there?"

"Uh-huh."

"I need to talk to her."

"Will you talk to me again?"

This whole situation was harder than he was letting on. "Austin, you and I are buddies." He wished the boy was within arm's reach. "Buddies always talk to each other. So get your mom and I'll tell her to call you to the phone when we're done."

"Okay." Jack heard the pleasure in the boy's voice before he yelled. "Mom!"

Grimacing, he pulled the receiver away from his ear. His son had hearty lungs. *His son.* Sometimes he felt as if he'd made this all up. It occurred to him one night after talking to Austin that he'd never expected to say those words, to have a son or daughter.

"Austin said you wanted to talk to me," Abby said in a questioning tone.

Jack didn't waste words. "Who's Uncle David?" he asked, not recalling Laura mentioning anyone by that name.

"My boss." Abby offered an explanation without a second thought. As Austin's father, he deserved to know where his son would be on the holiday. "He and his wife have an open house for anyone who doesn't have family for the holiday."

But she did. He didn't remind her of the obvious. A protest about not being with Austin for Thanksgiving nearly came out. With effort, he held it silent. If she wasn't ready to see him again, pushing her wouldn't do any good. "Nice."

"You'd like him." She frowned. Now, why had she said that?

"How are you doing?"

She coiled the telephone cord around a finger. "Fine." Had they come to the stage of only passing polite pleasantries. "And you?"

"Missing you, Abby." Confused. He'd meant what he'd said. He was settling down; he wanted to marry her; he wanted to give their son a real home. And she wouldn't believe in him.

Oh, Jack. She'd always be weak to him, she knew in that instant. Feeling Austin's stare, she made sure she didn't overreact. "Austin wants to talk to you."

Jack sat back on the edge of a chair and scowled at the phone. He'd gone slow, sending flowers, talking to her whenever he was waiting for Austin to take the phone. Hell, nothing was working. And if it were any other woman, he might believe she was playing hard to get or simply being stubborn. But Abby was too honest for one and too agreeable to do the other. She was resisting him because in her heart she believed that was best for everyone.

"Dad, are you listening?"

Jack jerked himself to attention. "I'm sorry, pal. What did you say?"

"My Cub Scout troop is having a spaghetti dinner for our dads. That means only dads can come. So do you want to go?"

"When exactly is it?" Jack asked. From Abby, Austin got a date. As he rattled it off, Jack winced. It was on a Monday night in October. The Friday to Sunday before the dinner, he was scheduled to purchase several horses in Montana.

"Can you come?"

"I'll try to come."

Austin whooped his pleasure. "I knew you would."

"Austin, I'll try," Jack repeated.

"Mom, he'd said he'd come." Austin grinned widely, hanging up the phone.

Sitting on the sofa, she set her pencil and crossword puzzle on the coffee table. Why was Jack agreeing to come? Annoyance stirred within her. He would hardly fly to Boston for one night to go to a Cub Scout dinner.

"Mom, are we going back to the ranch at Christmastime?"

Still fretting over the promise Jack had made, she turned a frown on Austin. "Why would you ask that?"

"Because Jason's dad lives in Colorado," he said about a friend at school, "and every Christmas he goes there to see him. And I wondered if I would do that, too."

Abby had to ask. "You liked it at the ranch, didn't you?"

Plopping down on the carpet in front of the television, he propped his elbow on the floor and braced his jaw on his knuckles. "Sure."

"To live there, you'd have to leave your school and friends."

Head down, he colored in his coloring book. "But Dad would be there. And you'd be there. We'd be a family."

Abby noticed his eyebrows had veed. How simple he made it all sound. She felt weak, willing. There was nothing more she would like to do than pack their suitcases, go back, take a chance. But how could she?

"You would be there, wouldn't you?"

Emotions close to the surface, Abby sought a diversion from a discussion she wasn't ready to have with him. On a short laugh, she pounced off the sofa cushion to him.

"Mom," he protested on a laughing wail while wiggling beneath her tickling fingers.

Just because he still let her do it, she tugged him close and gave him a wet kiss on the cheek.

"Mom!" he wailed again.

"Mom," she mimicked, and laughing, rolled him with her.

"Oh my gosh," he said suddenly, craning his neck to look toward the window.

Abby stilled with him in her arms. "What?"

"Look, Mom." His voice lifted with delight. "It's snowing."

She laughed at the sight of the large, white flakes and scrambled to a stand, pulling him up with her. "Let's go."

Chapter Thirteen

A bright orange glow broke the horizon. Jack stared for a moment at the rainbow of morning colors streaking the sky while cool, dry air chilled his face. Sounds of the ranch surrounded him—the snorting of horses, the earthy words of ranch hands, the bellowing of cattle. "It's snowing in Boston," he said, joining Sam by the corral fence.

Sam narrowed his eyes at the glare of the setting sun. "Bet Austin is enjoying himself." He regarded the ranch van leaving with guests for the airport.

"It was deep enough for them to make a snowman," Jack told him.

"I'll be back." He was already moving away to say goodbye to guests.

Snow. Snowmen. Halloween parties. Trick-or-treating. Every time Jack talked to Austin, he wished he was there.

"I told one of the guests about the snow in Boston," Sam said with his return. "He's from there."

"Did he moan?"

Sam cracked a smile. "He moaned. You know, if Austin moved here, he would miss the snow," he said, picking up on their previous conversation.

"I'd take him north so he could enjoy it." Jack leaned forward, draping his arms over the corral fence to watch Guy coaxing a skittish colt to accept a halter. "But chances of him ever living here aren't great."

"I thought you had persuasive powers," Sam teased.

Jack made fun of himself. "All the stories about me are myths."

"I doubt that. But—" A solemn, troubled expression pulled down his father's face. "I gather you're not having any luck convincing Abby they belong here, are you?"

What he was thinking came through loud and clear as Sam scowled and looked away. Jack placed a hand on his father's shoulder. "Dad, it's not your fault. We talked out everything that went wrong. She admitted she loved me."

He swung a look of surprise back at him. "Then why…?"

She doesn't trust me. "She insists I'm too much of a free spirit for them." He couldn't blame her. He'd lived a life that had revolved only around himself, around the next rodeo, another win. Was it any wonder that she had doubts he would be good for Austin, that she'd been hesitant to let him into Austin's life?

"But you aren't anymore." Sam nudged back his Stetson and scratched his head. "Didn't you tell her that you weren't going to rodeo?"

"Told her."

"She didn't believe you?"

Jack wound up the rope he'd been holding. "Didn't believe me," he admitted. He'd seriously thought about planting himself on her doorstep until she realized he wasn't going away this time, and until he convinced her that she couldn't live without him.

"What are you going to do about that?" Sam asked gruffly. "Her aunt wants Abby and the boy here. Me, too."

"Well, I'd sort of be glad, too, you know." Jack grinned at him. "If you have any ideas, let me know."

The week of the Cub Scout dinner, Boston was draped in white from a sudden and early winter storm. The temperature had plummeted and the heavy snowfall had bottled traffic. A gusting wind swirled around Abby when she trudged through snow after work.

For a short time on Monday afternoon, the day of the dinner, the airport had shut down, delaying planes. Wondering if Jack was still in Montana, she called her aunt while Austin was changing into his Cub Scout uniform.

"It's ninety, and unseasonably warm," her aunt told her after Abby lamented about the cold. "Jack is in Montana," she said, even though Abby hadn't asked.

What she wanted to know was if Jack had said anything about flying to Boston instead of to Phoenix, but she believed if he'd said anything, her aunt would have mentioned it.

So, after the phone call, Abby decided to prepare Austin for the possibility that Jack wouldn't come. "He had to go to Montana on business," she said to him while he was buttoning his shirt. She sounded like her mother.

Abby sat on the edge of Austin's bed. It was funny how something in the past sparked a memory. She recalled the night of a school play. She'd been ten, thrilled to have the lead part as Dorothy in an abbreviated version of *The Wizard of Oz*. When her father hadn't shown up, her mother had said similar words to her. "He had to go to work. His music is important to him," she'd said, sending Abby a disapproving look for expecting too much.

"He'll come, Mom," Austin said simply, snapping her from the memory.

Hadn't she been just as sure about her father until her mother had said that? Moving to the bedroom window, she watched light snowflakes dancing in the air. Fortunately, tonight's dinner was being held at a church hall a block from their apartment building. Taking control of the situation, Abby had talked to David, her boss, about his going with Austin. Only she'd yet to mention the idea to Austin.

Her mood drooping for her son, and with no dinner to make, she needed something to keep her busy. In the kitchen, she whipped up a batch of brownies, then placed the pan in the oven.

The chocolate smell of brownies permeated the kitchen. Sitting at the table, she played catch-up, reading the morning edition of the newspaper. She tried to concentrate on the crossword puzzle, read her horoscope, but she clock-watched. Seven o'clock came. Five minutes passed. Then ten.

From the other room, she heard Austin humming the theme song of his favorite television program. "It's snowing again, Mom," he said as he came into the kitchen to stand by the window.

He was dressed in his blue Cub Scout uniform. "Yes, I saw." She had to prepare him. "Austin, it's possible your dad won't get here. The weather is so bad," she said as an excuse.

"He'll come." He turned a disgruntled scowl on her for even expressing doubt. "He promised."

He's never liked making promises, she wanted to say, but she kept silent. How could she do anything to weaken such faith? Wasn't that what Jack had told her she needed? And wasn't this exactly the kind of moment that she'd hoped to protect her son from? "Austin, we'll be late if we don't leave."

His eyes shifted toward the window. He looked

torn, wanting to stay and wait for Jack, yet knowing he had to go now or miss the fun.

With the *ping* of the oven bell, Abby removed the brownie pan and set it on a rack to cool. "I'll call David, and he'll meet you—"

Shrugging into his parka, Austin shook his head. "I'll sit at Mr. Randall's table," he said about the scout leader.

"Austin, David said he'd come." She'd been appreciative that her boss and his wife had understood the problem she had. Though he'd already raised his own family, he'd been readily willing to help her.

It was clear that Austin would accept no substitute. He shot a look at her, one that told her no. It was a look she'd seen on Jack's face when annoyed. How often as their son grew toward manhood would she see a gesture or a look that reminded her of his father?

Abby said no more. While he zipped his blue parka, she pulled on boots, then slid on her jacket. In silence, they trudged through the snow. As snowflakes rushed down on them, Abby shoved gloved hands into her pockets. Near the church, they had to detour half a block because of knee-high snowdrifts.

Stepping ahead of Abby, Austin opened the door that led into the church hall. Her heart ached for him. Wasn't this what she'd longed to avoid? She'd never wanted him to feel the emptiness of waiting for a parent who never showed up. "I'll come back for you," she said.

Head down, he nodded while sliding out of his jacket.

Abby scanned the room of males. "There's Mr.—"

"Mom!" He shoved his jacket at her. "Mom, Dad's here!"

"What?" Abby searched a sea of faces, then she saw him. She saw him and still didn't believe it, but her heart filled.

Grinning, Jack strode toward them. As Austin leaped into his arms, he laughed at that and the stunned look on Abby's face. He gave Austin a long hug while he soaked up the sight of Abby. He loved the way she looked. A snowflake clung to a dark eyelash. From the cold, a rosiness colored her cheeks. And her smile nearly buckled his knees.

Too many empty hours had passed without both of them. He wanted to touch her, but wasn't sure he could set pride aside again. More than once, he'd reached out for her and had been rejected.

"Austin was so sure you'd be here." Abby smiled, Austin's delight rubbing off on her.

"Uh-huh. I knew you'd come," Austin piped in.

"I almost didn't make it on time. My connecting flight was delayed." His eyes coursed over her hair, fiery beneath the light. Pulled away from her face, the coppery strands were held in place with a barrette at the nape of her neck.

"When you didn't come to the apartment—"

"I knew I wouldn't get here on time if I went to

your apartment first. It's good you gave the church address the other night when we talked.''

She'd forgotten that she had and had assumed he wouldn't show when he hadn't arrived at the apartment.

During the walk here, she'd thought about his trip to Montana. Then she thought about what he was going to make her have to deal with because he'd made a promise he couldn't keep. She'd felt anger that she'd be the one who would have to comfort their son when Jack failed to show. She'd had no faith in him, Abby admitted.

''You face is cold,'' Jack said to Austin before setting him down.

An urge moved through Abby to step closer, touch Jack's cheek. He looked cold, too. The collar of his jacket was still raised, and snow dusted his shoulders and hair, indicating he'd arrived only minutes before them.

''I don't know how you stand this weather.'' Through a blinding curtain of snow, Jack had seen cars buried to their tires in snowdrifts during the drive from the airport. When his cab had gotten stuck in one, he'd walked two blocks before he'd connected with another one.

''Three layers of clothes in winter,'' Abby said on a laugh. ''I'm glad you got here.''

''As soon as I arrived, I called your place.'' Jack gestured with his thumb behind him and toward the public telephones. ''But you'd left.'' God, but he'd missed her.

"Mom, I'm going by Jason." Austin indicated the boy waving at him. "Are you coming, Dad?"

For a moment longer, he kept his eyes on Abby. "I'll be there in a minute. Save me a seat at a table."

"I will."

Abby waited until Austin was out of hearing range. "Thank you for coming tonight, Jack."

"I don't need a thank-you. He's my son. Abby, nothing would keep me from Austin now that I know he's mine. I meant it when I told you that I was staying in his life. And in yours." A look of frustration knit his forehead. "Why don't you believe me? Why did you think I wouldn't come?"

She couldn't lie. "I thought you'd get busy with your own life. I thought once Austin was out of sight, you'd forget he exists."

"What?" Jack leveled a hard look at her. That hurt. Did she really believe he was so selfish, so insensitive? He could understand that she found it hard to believe he'd give up rodeo, but he'd never done anything to lead her to believe he'd be so thoughtless with Austin. "I don't deserve that. I never gave you any reason to believe that. Did I?"

Abby stared dumbfounded at him. "No." No, he hadn't, so why had she said that? Another man had done that, she reflected. He'd walked away without a look back and had left a little girl heartbroken.

"I wouldn't do that to him," Jack said with a trace of anger edging his voice. "I meant it when I said that I planned to be here for him."

Confusion more than doubts overwhelmed her. What had she done? Those words hung in her mind.

"Mom, we got to go for the food," Austin insisted, suddenly beside them again.

Silent, she felt unsteady from her own thoughts. Aware of Austin's quizzical stare, she took her cue. He was eager to join the others, she knew, show off his dad, the cowboy. Though, except for his boots, Jack looked no different than the other fathers who were wearing Levi's. "I should leave." She shifted toward Austin, touching his back for a goodbye. "Have a good time."

Without looking back, troubled now, she walked to the exit.

Shuffling her booted feet through the snow on the sidewalk, she raised her face, letting the cold wind caress her cheeks. But she didn't remember the walk home or unlocking the door. Inside the apartment, despite the warmth, she felt cold. Keeping her jacket on, she stared out the living-room window for a long time and watched the snowflakes fall.

She'd thought she was protecting Austin from the hurt, the disappointment, the heartache he would feel if Jack let him down, if Jack abandoned Austin when he tired of playing daddy.

All along she'd believed, truly believed, that she only wanted to protect Austin. But from what was the big question. Jack had given Austin a father who loved and cared about him, who'd sit for an hour on the phone discussing a comic-book character or a Halloween costume. He'd given him a father who made a promise and kept it. Austin hadn't needed protection from heartbreak.

Squeezing her eyes tight, she agonized. This wasn't about Jack. This was about her father. When—when had her past gotten mixed up with her feelings for Jack? Why had it? On a long breath, she let the pain of honesty surge through her. She hadn't been protecting Austin. She'd been protecting herself. If she didn't believe in Jack, didn't let herself accept him in her life, she didn't risk being left again. She could keep herself safe.

She steadied herself with a long breath and finally stood. After removing her jacket, she wandered into the kitchen. She'd just set up the coffeemaker when behind her she heard the sound of muffled voices, then the click of the door opening.

"Mom, we're home." Austin rushed in, a scarf dangling from his hand. He frowned but said nothing about the door being unlocked.

So much needed to be said, Abby realized as she went through motions for Austin. She smiled at her son, bent down to kiss his cheek, even helped him remove his jacket before she made herself meet Jack's eyes. She saw hurt in them and knew she was causing it.

Head bent, Austin unzipped his jacket. "Mom, we had so much fun."

She looked at Jack instead of him. "You, too?"

"Me, too," he answered easily. No matter what happened now, he didn't regret coming, having this time with his son.

''We had a pie-eating contest.'' Austin dropped a glove on the table, a scarf on the sofa.

Abby noticed Jack hadn't left the doorway. He seemed more distant. Could she blame him? She'd been unfair. Terribly unfair. ''What kind of pie?''

''Lemon meringue.''

She frowned at the trail of clothes he was leaving behind him. ''You are picking all of them up, aren't you?'' she asked, pointing a finger at his discarded scarf and gloves.

As if he'd been asked to do something above and beyond the norm, he released a heavy sigh, but he did as expected and gathered up his clothes. ''I'll put them away,'' he said before she could. Starting for his room, he stopped in midstride. ''You haven't seen my room, Dad. Want to?''

You're here for Austin, Jack reminded himself. After what had happened earlier, for the first time since she'd left the ranch, he had doubts they could heal what was wrong between them. Not sure what to do about her, he did nothing. Instead, he gave Austin his attention. ''Sure, I'd like to see it.'' He'd already scanned the apartment. Neat but not immaculate, it was decorated in a homespun country look. ''Lead the way.'' Following Austin, he unzipped his jacket.

Clearly, Abby had worked hard to make the room a comfortable haven for Austin. From the dark blue ceiling with its painted stars to the posters of Captain Cosmo and the bedspread with its spaceship design, the room suited Austin perfectly.

"Do you like it?" Austin's eyes were steady on him as if the future of the world rested on his answer.

"Sure do." At the barn, waiting for the boy, was a bigger room with a view of the mountains, but without Abby's touch, it would never be a home to Austin.

"Want to see something else?" He grabbed Jack's hand. "We got to go back to the other room."

As they left the bedroom, Austin released Jack's hand and rushed across the living room. Jack stopped in the bedroom doorway to watch Abby, hunting for something in a laundry basket of unfolded clothes. "I like your apartment."

"Thank you," she replied. The world narrowed to the small space separating them. The ball was in her court, she knew.

"Do you want to see the scrapbook?" Austin cut in.

Scrapbook? Abby swung around to see him opening the entertainment-center cabinet. She hadn't realized he even knew she'd done the scrapbook of newspaper and magazine clippings about Jack.

"It's a scrapbook all about you," Austin said while lifting the book. "I found it yesterday."

It took a moment for Jack to grasp what he was talking about. By then, Austin was holding the leather-bound book out to him. He felt a catch in his heart as he opened the book, as he skimmed the pages filled with clippings. They began when he'd been in an Arizona rodeo during that first summer with Abby. "This is nice," he said, noticing she even had several articles about the last rodeo he'd performed in.

Abby knew that no denying would work. The scrapbook symbolized that he'd always been a part of her life, always would be, unless she kept acting like a fool. In his hands was a token of the love that had started when she'd been much younger, still filled with expectations.

Jack set the book down. When he'd come, it had been for Austin. He hadn't been sure after all these months if there was any chance for him and Abby. But he still ached for her, still longed to have her in his arms. Aware of Austin standing near, he took control of the moment, deciding he and Abby needed privacy. "Austin, why don't you find that trading card of Qwiwala," he said about one of Captain Cosmo's buddies.

"You want to see it?"

Jack kept his hand on the scrapbook. Its very existence touched him. "I'd really like to," he said, not taking his eyes off Abby. He couldn't let her pull away from him again.

"Be right back."

Abby watched Austin dash into his room. They wouldn't have a lot of time alone.

"I've been so wrong," she began. How could she explain her own confusion? "You'd done everything you could to prove you meant what you'd said, that you were staying at the ranch." She steadied herself with a long breath. "You'd offered me marriage and a home for our son, everything I could want. And still I kept expecting you to let him down." Her heart quickened to a light, fluttery beat with her steps toward him. "But this wasn't about you. That's what I didn't understand. This was about my father. I never forgave or forgot what my father did to me and my mother."

He hadn't expected those words. Jack brushed a strand of hair away from her cheek.

It would have been so easy to fall into his arms and say no more, but she knew she couldn't do that. "I guess I've been trying to protect myself from the kind of hurt I felt when he wasn't around anymore." A look of understanding in his eyes encouraged her to go on. "After he left us, she—we followed him. My mother moved us around. Wherever he went, wherever he got a job playing with a band, we would go. I doubt he even knew we were near. I don't know what she thought would happen. Maybe she believed if we were close, then he could come back at any time."

She paused, but now wasn't the time to falter. "She never gave up. Foolishly. She never stopped hoping he'd come back to us." Abby recalled nights when she'd heard her mother crying. "She kept saying that he'd promised to come back. I wonder now if he ever did promise. Maybe she just kept hoping. I don't know. But I knew that I never wanted to go through that again, never would let myself be left again. Then I did. With you."

Jack's gut clenched. *Oh, God, what he'd done to her.* It all made more sense to him now. She'd known a childhood with a woman who never let her forget that the man they'd loved had left them. And then he'd done the same thing. So when he'd finally gotten his head on straight and wanted what Abby did, she was afraid to believe in him, believe in them.

"It hurt so badly," she admitted. Jack's leaving had forced too many painful memories on her of that time in her life. "Jack, she never let go of the past and neither had I. I kept letting it control my life."

He didn't need her to say more. He saw in the moist darkness of her eyes the warmth of love. "Come here." As Abby took another step, he dragged her closer. "I love you. I always have."

Abby released the breath she hadn't known she'd been holding. "And I love you." She trembled with emotion, closing her eyes and absorbing the feel of his arms around her, the heat of his mouth on hers. Her heart open and welcoming, she pressed her cheek to his, and she clung. "And I'm sorry. I'm so—so sorry. Jack, I don't want to live in the past anymore. I want to think about now, tomorrow with Austin—and you, if you still want both of us."

He smiled in a wry, familiar way that tugged at her heart. "How could you even doubt that?" He'd spent some lonely nights awake in his bed, staring at the ceiling, trying to figure out what went wrong. He'd never planned to give up. His son and the woman he loved belonged with him. But for a while, he'd been stymied about how to make that happen.

In the blue eyes staring down at her, she saw the truth in his words. "I'm lucky you're so stubborn. Any other man would have given up on me by now. And I'd have lost so much." Need swarming in on her, she met his mouth again. Long and deep, the kiss bound them, and in the lips moving over hers, she felt the tenderness and the love that she'd blocked from her heart for too long.

With emotion flooding him, Jack forced himself to ease back before he forgot where they were and how close Austin was. "Tell me what you want."

Abby spoke from her heart as joy hummed through her. "You," she whispered close to his mouth.

Jack released a laugh. "I'd like to believe that's all you need to make you happy, but let's get serious."

The solemn look on his face stirred her smile.

Tempted by silky strands, Jack toyed with one curving her jaw. He wanted her to spell it out, needed a confirmation that all he'd hoped for with her would be a reality. "Will you marry me?"

Abby didn't hesitate. "Yes, yes," she said, giving him a quick kiss between her laughter.

"I know it's a lot to ask of you. But I have to stay at the ranch. I have responsibilities there."

"Austin said he misses the rooster."

Jack returned her smile. He wanted her to see the same future he'd begun to imagine, but she deserved to have all she wanted, too. "I know the local news-paper is small-time compared to the one you work on, but Orlon would probably be thrilled to have someone with your experience."

She knew that was true. Orlon had even offered her a position.

"Or you could write a book," he added. "You said you'd like to do that someday. Remember?"

He'd stunned her. She'd mentioned that only once, eight years ago.

"Whatever you decide is all right with me."

"I'll figure that out later." Abby traced his lips with a fingertip. His smile slowly formed, but he was looking past her. With a glance back over her shoulder, she saw Austin peeking out of the bed-room.

Keeping his one arm around Abby's waist, Jack opened his other arm to his son. Austin's eyes wid-ened, then without a word spoken, he dashed to them. They were complete now, Jack thought as he caught Austin at the waist and lifted him up. "This time's forever, Abby."

Her heart pounding, she let the softness of his voice and those words float over her. *Yes, forever.*

"We have only one thing to do before we go home," he said to both of them.

Happiness bubbling within her, Abby glanced at Austin, wondering if he knew what Jack was talking about. He looked as puzzled as she was. "What's that?"

Jack winked at her, then met his son's eyes. "We need to pick up a dog."

"A dog!" Austin's voice raised an octave. "A real dog?"

"A puppy," Jack suggested, because then the dog would be Austin's and grow with him.

Exhilaration squeaked his young voice. "A puppy! A puppy, Mom. We're going to get a puppy. Is that great?"

Laughing, she coiled an arm around Jack's neck. "Perfect."

"He wants a baby brother, too," Jack murmured.

Surprised, Abby drew back. "A brother?"

Jack grinned. "What do you think of that idea?"

Abby didn't hesitate. "I love the idea."

With the sound of her son's giggle in her ear, she pressed her mouth to Jack's for a kiss. In it, she felt passion. And she felt a promise of forever.

*   *   *   *   *

Silhouette®SPECIAL EDITION®
LINDSAY McKENNA
delivers two more exciting books in her heart-stopping new series:

MORGAN'S MERCENARIES
III
THE HUNTERS

Coming in July 1999:
HUNTER'S WOMAN
Special Edition #1255

Ty Hunter wanted his woman back from the moment he set his piercing gaze on her. For despite the protest on Dr. Catt Alborak's soft lips, Ty was on a mission to give the stubborn beauty everything he'd foolishly denied her once—his heart, his soul—and most of all, his child....

And coming in October 1999:
HUNTER'S PRIDE
Special Edition #1274

Devlin Hunter had a way with the ladies, but when it came to his job as a mercenary, the brooding bachelor worked alone. Until his latest assignment paired him up with Kulani Dawson, a feisty beauty whose tender vulnerabilities brought out his every protective instinct—and chipped away at his proud vow to never fall in love....

Look for the exciting series finale in early 2000—when MORGAN'S MERCENARIES: THE HUNTERS comes to Silhouette Desire®!

Available at your favorite retail outlet.

SILHOUETTE BOOKS
is proud to announce the arrival of

THE BABY OF THE MONTH CLUB:

the latest installment of author
Marie Ferrarella's
popular miniseries.

When pregnant Juliette St. Claire met Gabriel Saldana than she discovered he wasn't the struggling artist he claimed to be. An undercover agent, Gabriel had been sent to Juliette's gallery to nab his prime suspect: Juliette herself. But when he discovered her innocence, would he win back Juliette's heart and convince her that he was the daddy her baby needed?

Don't miss Juliette's induction into
THE BABY OF THE MONTH CLUB
in September 1999.
Available at your favorite retail outlet.

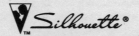

FOR THE CHILDREN

Sometimes families are made in the most unexpected ways!

Don't miss this heartwarming new series from
Silhouette Special Edition®, Silhouette Romance®
and popular author

DIANA WHITNEY

Every time matchmaking lawyer
Clementine Allister St. Ives brings a couple
together, it's for the children...
and sure to bring romance!

August 1999
I NOW PRONOUNCE YOU MOM & DAD
Silhouette Special Edition #1261
Ex-lovers Powell Greer and Lydia Farnsworth knew *nothing*
about babies, but Clementine said they needed to learn—fast!

September 1999
A DAD OF HIS OWN
Silhouette Romance #1392
When Clementine helped little Bobby find his father, Nick Purcell
appeared on the doorstep. Trouble was, Nick wasn't Bobby's dad!

October 1999
THE FATHERHOOD FACTOR
Silhouette Special Edition #1276
Deirdre O'Connor's temporary assignment from Clementine
involved her handsome new neighbor, Ethan Devlin—and
adorable twin toddlers!

Available at your favorite retail outlet.

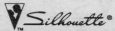

Silhouette®

Look us up on-line at: http://www.romance.net   SSEFTC

"Fascinating—you'll want to take this home!"
—**Marie Ferrarella**

"Each page is filled with a brand-new surprise."
—**Suzanne Brockmann**

"Makes reading a new and joyous experience all over again."
—**Tara Taylor Quinn**

See what all your favorite authors are talking about.

Coming October 1999 to a retail store near you.

THE
FORTUNES
OF TEXAS™

This BRAND-NEW program includes 12 incredible stories about a wealthy Texas family rocked by scandal and embedded in mystery.

It is based on the tremendously successful *Fortune's Children* continuity.

Membership in this family has its privileges…and its price.

But what a fortune can't buy, a true-bred Texas love is sure to bring!

This exciting program will start in September 1999!

Available at your favorite retail outlet.

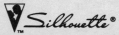

Silhouette®

Coming this September 1999
from SILHOUETTE BOOKS
and bestselling author

RACHEL LEE

CONARD COUNTY:
Boots & Badges

Alicia Dreyfus—a desperate woman on the run—
is about to discover that she *can* come home
again...to Conard County. Along the way she
meets the man of her dreams—and brings together
three other couples, whose love blossoms beneath
the bold Wyoming sky.

Enjoy four complete, **brand-new** stories in one
extraordinary volume.

Available at your favorite retail outlet.

Silhouette ® SPECIAL EDITION ®

presents **THE BRIDAL CIRCLE**, a brand-new
miniseries honoring friendship, family and love...

THE BRIDAL CIRCLE

by
Andrea Edwards

**They dreamed of marrying and leaving their
small town behind—but soon discovered there's
no place like home for true love!**

IF I ONLY HAD A...HUSBAND (May '99)
Penny Donnelly had tried desperately to forget charming
millionaire Brad Corrigan. But her heart had a memory—and a
will—of its own. And Penny's heart was set on Brad becoming
her husband....

SECRET AGENT GROOM (August '99)
When shy-but-sexy Heather Mahoney bumbles onto secret agent
Alex Waterstone's undercover mission, the only way to protect the
innocent beauty is to claim her as his lady love. Will Heather
carry out her own secret agenda and claim Alex as her groom?

PREGNANT & PRACTICALLY MARRIED
(November '99)
Pregnant Karin Spencer had suddenly lost her memory and
gained a pretend fiancé. Though their match was make-believe,
Jed McCarron was her dream man. Could this bronco-bustin'
cowboy give up his rodeo days for family ways?

Available at your favorite retail outlet.

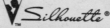
Silhouette ®